He was close enough to see the tears streaming down her cheeks.

Ah, hell. He hadn't meant to cause that.

"You want to know what my life was like?" she pushed.

"Imagine the worst day you've ever had..." Her eyes were wild; he'd never seen her like this before. "And then imagine people were getting hurt all around you and you had no power to stop it."

"Tell me what he did to you, Melissa," he said. He needed to hear the words.

"Right now all I can think about is staying alive so that I can take care of my little girl. I get that you hate me. I hurt you and I probably deserve whatever anger you hurl at me. But my life has been hell and I just want this nightmare to end. Nothing else matters until it does."

Colin couldn't think of one positive thing to say to calm her down so he threw all caution to the wind, pulled her into his arms and kissed her.

TEXAS WITNESS

USA TODAY Bestselling Author
BARB HAN

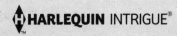
HARLEQUIN INTRIGUE®

Many thanks go to Allison Lyons, who makes every book better! A deep well of gratitude
goes to Jill Marsal, who really is the best of the best and a dream to work with.

Brandon, Jacob and Tori, the three of you light up my life in so many bright and colorful
ways. I love each of you even more with every passing year, and it is my greatest pleasure
to see the beautiful people you've become.

Babe, we're watching another one of our babies test his wings. We get to enjoy a few more
years with our youngest before she does the same. Then it'll be the two of us again, just
like in the beginning… And a whole new set of adventures await. I love you!

ISBN-13: 978-0-373-75700-8

Texas Witness

Copyright © 2017 by Barb Han

Recycling programs
for this product may
not exist in your area.

Printed in U.S.A.

H HARLEQUIN®
™ www.Harlequin.com

USA TODAY bestselling author **Barb Han** lives in north Texas with her very own hero-worthy husband, three beautiful children, a spunky golden retriever/standard poodle mix and too many books in her to-read pile. In her downtime, she plays video games and spends much of her time on or around a basketball court. She loves interacting with readers and is grateful for their support. You can reach her at barbhan.com.

Books by Barb Han

Harlequin Intrigue

Cattlemen Crime Club

Stockyard Snatching
Delivering Justice
One Tough Texan
Texas-Sized Trouble
Texas Witness

Mason Ridge

Texas Prey
Texas Takedown
Texas Hunt
Texan's Baby

The Campbells of Creek Bend

Witness Protection
Gut Instinct
Hard Target

Rancher Rescue

Harlequin Intrigue Noir

Atomic Beauty

Visit the Author Profile page at Harlequin.com.

CAST OF CHARACTERS

Melissa Roark Rancic—Marrying the wrong man and pretending he's the father of her child seemed like the only way out of a desperate situation. But her deception is turning on her and she has no place left to run.

Colin O'Brien—The fourth of six O'Brien boys. He's still feeling the sting from the day Melissa tossed his engagement ring at him and ran off with another man. When she shows up at his family's Spring Fling, he's there to make sure she knows she's not welcome.

Angelina Rancic—This infant is an O'Brien through and through, even if her mother tries to hide her paternity in order to save her life.

Richard Rancic—A soon-to-be ex who refuses to let Melissa go. He's on the run from the law and will do anything to take back his child and get revenge against a wife who betrayed him by turning state's witness.

Raymond Rancic—This brother is involved in criminal activity up to his neck.

Marshal Davis—Is he really dead? Or is he involved?

Tommy Johnson—The sheriff who grew up at the O'Brien ranch and considers them family. When he's shot it's easy to see how far Rancic will go for revenge.

hands in the air, worry lines bracketing her mouth. She'd worked at the ranch for a little more than five years. She'd become close with his family and knew that the subject of Melissa was off-limits. "Honest. I thought she moved away a year ago. I had no idea she'd resurface."

"She did." The thought that she'd returned to Bluff, Texas, let alone be bold enough to show up at his family's fund-raiser riding on someone else's invitation, sat hot and heavy. The heels of his boots clicked on the tile floor as he paced. The last time he'd seen her had been when she'd handed him the engagement ring she'd been wearing—the one he'd given her— and then married one of the biggest jerks to ever blow through town, Richard Rancic. The guy was all flash and no substance, splashing local businesses with his money before taking what he wanted—Melissa—and breezing out of town. The newlyweds had disappeared after the quickie wedding. Apparently, Melissa couldn't get away from Colin fast enough.

He'd moved on, dated plenty of interesting women since then. The thought of seeing her again shouldn't hurt this much. And just to prove to himself that it didn't, he planned to march right into the ballroom and show her just how freakin' fantastic he was doing since she'd told him that she didn't love him the same anymore and then walked out of his life.

Cynthia stalked toward the kitchen table, where Colin had seen her cell phone.

"I'm calling security. Don't worry about a thing. You don't even have to look at her. I'll have her escorted out. She shouldn't be here and Carolina should've known better than to bring her. I'm putting them both on the Never Allow list." Her voice had that *shaming* quality.

"No need. I'll walk her out myself and then deal with Carolina personally," Colin bit out in a low growl.

Cynthia tensed, reacting to his sharp words.

Well, he hadn't meant to make her do that. He'd apologize later. Right now, he had an important matter to take care of. He didn't want one of his brothers seeing Melissa first and ushering her out of the building before he got a chance to have his say. No, he wanted to handle this little *problem* on his own. Carolina might've been Melissa's girlfriend but she'd become close with his family. Colin considered Carolina a friend, too, until now.

Colin stalked out of the room and toward the Great Hall. The place was decorated to the nines for the Spring Fling. Paper lanterns hung from the forty-foot tented ceiling. White candles contrasted against the dark oak beams and wood floors. Round tables with white linens covering them surrounded the dance floor. The place, fixed up, gave a nod to its heritage as an old horse barn and had rustic charm in spades.

Colin's blood pressure spiked with each step inside the room as he searched for his target. George Strait's "Baby Blue" filled the air as pairs of boots shuffled around the dance floor in a two-step.

And then he saw her. His gaze fixed. His heart fisted.

Melissa Rancic stood in front of the buffet table, nervously searching the faces in the crowd. At least she had enough sense to be worried even if she also had a whole helluva lot of nerve showing up at his family home.

Colin didn't want to acknowledge how damn good she looked. Her wavy auburn hair hung just past her shoulders. She'd cut it since the last time he'd seen her when it fell mid-back in large ringlets. She had on a cream-colored sleeveless dress that smoothed along the soft curves of her frame and flared below the waist with two layers of ruffles.

The dress fell mid-thigh, showing off those long legs of hers. Her fingers toyed with the necklace that hung in the middle of her chest, and the huge rock on her wedding finger sparkled in the dim light. She wore light brown boots with blue inlay. The fact that she still owned them at all made him believe she'd stayed somewhere in Texas. Although, she could live anywhere. He wouldn't know. After the way she'd left things unfinished between them, he'd refused to talk about her again. She'd made her choice and he'd closed up inside, telling himself that he needed to cowboy up and move on. Of course, he'd spent plenty of couch time licking his wounds before he'd had enough of the lovesick-puppy routine.

Memories of her in his arms, her warm, naked skin against his, tried to break through his thoughts as he stared at her. The way she smelled like early morning on a sunny day in spring, all flowers and warmth. Her intelligence. The way she laughed…

Those thoughts had about as much place in his mind as she had in his house. To be clear, there was room for neither. It was about time she knew it.

As he stalked closer, he realized there was more than worry going on in her head. She was anxious, stressed and those weren't the same things. She had to know this was the last place on earth she should be. Since it had been so easy for her to walk away from him last year and shut him out of her life completely, he figured her apprehension had nothing to do with the possibility of running into him. Was she afraid Carolina had disappeared on her? She was looking for someone. Or *looking out* for someone. Watching. Weary.

Her weight shifted from side to side like when she was nervous. She kept toying with that necklace, too. Was that a gift from *him*, from Richard?

Rather than sneak up on her or come at her from the side, Colin took a straight-on approach, and he didn't bother to hide the intensity in his glare. If she had the guts to come to his house, she could take it.

The second she saw him, her body language changed. Her posture tensed and she stood stiff and uncomfortable. A look of panic crossed her features as her gaze darted around, probably looking for an escape route. With the buffet table behind her and the only other exit to Colin's back, she was trapped in between.

As he neared, he could see that her pulse pounded at the base of her neck—a neck he had no business looking at in the first place, especially not the exact spot that made her mewl with pleasure when his mouth covered it.

When he was close enough to see the violet streaks in her brown eyes, she tried to duck right.

"Not so fast," Colin ground out, catching her by the arm.

"Let go of me, Colin O'Brien," she said, facing toward the east wall, refusing to look at him directly.

Colin wasn't about to let her get away with that. It was high time she learned that sidestepping a problem didn't make it go away. He spun her around to face him. They were almost nose-to-nose and the movement brought her scent washing over him, memories crashing into him. His heart double fisted.

"Why are you here?" he managed to bite out, clenching his back teeth.

"I shouldn't have come." Her eyes were pleading for him to let go now.

He couldn't. He wanted—no, *needed* to understand what he'd done wrong to make her run out on him in the first place. His pride kept him from asking as she shook out of his grip, the diamond on her wedding ring scratching his arm as she jerked free.

"Hold on, Mel—"

Before he could finish, she was gone. She'd dashed across the dance floor, pushed open the double doors to the lawn and fled. All the lines he'd practiced in his head a million times over were a distant memory. He stood there, mute and stupid. Frozen. Just like before.

Dancing had stopped even though the music played on. All eyes were on him now. From his peripheral vision, he saw two of his brothers making a beeline toward him.

Colin wasn't in the mood for a family meeting, so he reversed course and then ditched them out the back door.

HEART POUNDING, MELISSA ran to her sedan. She should've known better than to show up at the O'Brien's ranch. Yet, she'd had to see Colin one more time before disappearing into her new identity in witness protection. She glanced at the clock on her dashboard. She had little more than two hours left before saying goodbye to her past life. At midnight, Melissa Rancic would no longer exist. Richard Rancic, her husband and a hardened criminal, had escaped custody and was on the loose. According to her US marshal handler, Tim Davis, Richard was last seen making a run for the Canadian border. That he was so far away had given her the confidence she'd needed to come back to Bluff and see Colin. She'd expected it to hurt but also to comfort her. To give her the strength she would need to do what had to be done in order to protect her daughter.

Hands shaking, she managed to retrieve her purse from the backseat and locate her keys. Getting the right one in the ignition proved a frustrating challenge. After several attempts, she had the engine purring and the Great Hall in the rearview. Not long after that, the entire O'Brien ranch disappeared.

Head spinning, she thought about the fact that Colin hadn't changed one bit, unless it was possible to look even better. That old saying about absence making the heart grow fonder proved true. His jet-black hair and those intense dark eyes still had the power to make her weak-kneed with one look. There was a deeper emotion present in his eyes now, too, and it looked a lot like hurt.

The past year of living without him had been like living in an Arctic cave…brutal, dark, cold. There'd been no sun. No laughter. No joy. And yet, day after day, she'd had to put on a brave face with her husband and pretend that she loved him. Both her and her daughter's survival had depended on delivering a good show. A shiver raced through her as she thought about what her life had turned into and the dangerous man she was running from.

Life, like spring weather in Texas, could change in a flash.

The gravity of just how big a mistake it

had been to come back to Bluff, to see Colin, had shifted the ground beneath her feet. This whole idea had been a stupid mistake no matter how badly her body had reacted at the thought of never seeing him again, and the panic attack had been almost crippling. Her chest had squeezed until she thought it might burst. When release finally came, her heart filled with an ache so deep she could scarcely breathe.

Even so, it had been rash of her to think that she could get away with slipping into the dimly lit Great Hall and catch one last glimpse of him before someone recognized her and kicked her out. Based on his expression, he would have her thrown out himself.

Memories of spending time at the ranch assaulted her. She and Colin had been so happy, so carefree, so in love…

A sob escaped before she could suppress it. Her eyes blurred as she navigated onto the main road into town. At least she had their daughter. She'd have to hold on to that piece of Colin for the rest of her life and let it be enough. Angelina touched a piece of Melissa's heart that could belong to no one else. She thought about how unfair it was that her daughter had never met her real father, would never meet him.

But then, this was the way it had to be, she reminded herself. Melissa's father was old and sick. He'd made his mistakes and they were both paying for them. If Richard had followed through on his threats, her father would live out the rest of his life in jail. She couldn't allow that to happen no matter how angry she'd become at him for his unethical business practices. And then there were the threats Richard had made about Colin and his family. The man could destroy the O'Briens if their secret was revealed. The bedrock of the family had been their parents' unwavering love and devotion. If Richard had gone public with the photos he had, the ones of Mr. O'Brien having an affair, the family would've been crushed. Colin would've been devastated.

In order to save her father and Colin, Melissa had done as Richard had said. Break off her engagement with Colin and agree to marry Richard instead. Save two families. Melissa had naively believed that all she needed was time to figure out how to back out of the arrangement with Richard. It had all come at her so fast. How simple had she been to think that man wouldn't force her to go through with the wedding or a loveless union?

And then she'd missed her period. Once she'd realized she was pregnant and that Richard would stop at nothing to destroy her if she walked out on him, she'd been too frightened to put up a fight. Scared he'd force her to give the baby up for adoption or, worse yet, do something more sinister, she'd convinced Richard that Angelina was his. She hadn't realized how a small snowball of a lie could grow and build, gaining momentum until it became an avalanche and destroyed everything in its path, destroyed her.

In her heart, she'd known all along that Richard would've moved heaven and earth to find her if she'd left him before the feds became involved. Then he'd destroy everything she loved. The worst part about her whole marriage was that she'd had to persuade her husband that Colin meant nothing to her. Her and her daughter's lives had depended on Melissa being convincing.

Three days after Angelina had been born, the feds had shown up and told Melissa they were building a case against Richard and his family. She'd been given an ultimatum: help the government or lose her daughter. She'd negotiated to have her father taken into protective custody. He was living in an undisclosed facility. Melissa had secretly helped gather evidence against her husband, living in daily fear of being discovered. And that wasn't the worst of it. The true hell that she'd lived had been wondering what her life would have been like if she'd married Colin instead…

There was no time for doubts now.

Melissa had done what she'd had to do in order to protect those closest to her, including him. Regretting the past or her actions now wouldn't change a thing. Witnessing the pain in Colin's eyes had her second-guessing everything.

Tears streaked her cheeks as, once again, she drove away from the only man she'd ever loved.

Chapter Two

"Thank you so much, Mrs. Klein," Melissa said as she held out a couple of twenties in her fist, not realizing she was clenching her hand until she noticed her white knuckles.

The older woman glanced at Melissa and smiled before waving her hand. She'd retired and moved to Bluff after thirty years of teaching in the Houston ISD. Her husband's family was originally from the area, and the two of them had returned to live out their retirement in a small town. She was the perfect neighbor because she didn't know everyone yet and had no idea about Melissa's past in Bluff.

"I can't take all that and especially not for—" Mrs. Klein glanced at her watch "—an hour and fifteen minutes' worth of work."

"Please do. I didn't realize I'd be back so soon and I've messed up your whole evening." Tears free-fell down Melissa's cheeks now, and they had nothing to do with the words coming out of her mouth.

"Don't worry about it, dear. Seriously. There's still time to catch CSI with Bernard if I hurry." Mrs. Klein's brow furrowed and she had a mix of pity and kindness on her face. She really was a sweet woman. "The baby was no trouble. She's been asleep the whole time."

Melissa told herself to get it together. She would. It had been easier to leave town when she thought she was saving everyone she loved. With everything that she'd been through in the past twelve months, she figured she could endure most anything. Seeing Colin again was too much. She'd been naive to think that she could see him again and then walk away a second time without a few tears. He looked good…unbelievably good. Different, but good. His quick smile and easygoing charm had been replaced by distrust and cautious eyes.

The way he'd looked at her, so angry, so hurt…so final.

For Colin, there wasn't a lot of gray area. Life was black-and-white. She should've known that once she'd left him, he'd be done. Having her fear confirmed hurt. The only consolation was that she'd always have a piece of Colin with her in their daughter.

"At least take something for your time," Melissa managed to get out before Mrs. Klein could walk out the door.

Melissa flipped on the front porch light. Nothing happened. The electricity in this old house was about as reliable as the cell coverage in town. Both were spotty.

"Oh, great. Now what?" Melissa asked rhetorically as more tears streamed.

"It's really okay, dear. Don't make yourself sick over it," Mrs. Klein said, patting Melissa on the shoulder. "Are you going to be all right?"

Melissa suppressed a sob. "I'll be fine. It's been a long day and I just need a good night of sleep. That's all."

She wished a few hours of rest could fix all her problems. Instead, she'd be meeting with her handler in a little more than an hour and a half. Her world would never be the same again.

"Whatever's going on will get better with time. I promise," Mrs. Klein soothed.

The woman had no idea how complicated Melissa's life had become.

"At least take something for your trouble." Melissa held out the fistful of twenties toward Mrs. Klein.

"If it'll make you feel better." The old woman peeled off the top twenty and tucked it inside her pocket. She winked. "I'll take Bernard out to breakfast with that money in the morning."

"Thank you for everything," Melissa said. She closed and locked the door after watching Mrs. Klein walk across the street to see that she was safely home. She texted Carolina that she'd left the party.

Melissa was relieved that the older woman hadn't pressed to find out what was really wrong with her. She'd been mute for twelve long months, save for the conversations she'd had with the feds, and she wanted to shout from the rooftops now that she was free. But she wasn't really free. Richard was still out there. Somewhere. Melissa shivered at the thought. She was about to leave everything she'd ever known behind for witness protection because of that man. And there was a very real possibility that she would never see Colin again. A sob tried to escape. She suppressed it.

The feds had said that Richard should be somewhere near the Canadian border by now. Melissa had been under so much duress, especially in the past two months since talking with the agents, that she could barely think straight. She told herself that was the reason she'd been misguided enough to think seeing Colin one more time would somehow fill the ache in her chest.

Everything had spun out of control. Her relationship with the feds hadn't exactly been a friendly alliance. The only reason she'd collected evidence against Richard was because they threatened to take Angelina away from her. Ever since they'd approached her while she picked up the mail that cold January morning, she'd been walking a tightrope.

Richard had been good at covering his tracks, so culling evidence against him had been difficult. She'd eventually gathered the proof needed for the feds to get an arrest warrant. She'd risked her life, not to mention her daughter's. And what had they done with Richard? Allowed him to escape. No one could save Melissa now if Richard got to her. If it wasn't for Angelina, for that smiling angelic face, Melissa would've lost hope a long time ago.

Melissa was weary, lonely, and part of her felt like she'd never live a normal life again. At least her father was in protective custody. His health was sketchy but he was in a decent facility in the Pacific Northwest. That's the only information she'd been given and that's all she needed to know. She wasn't ready to forgive her father for what he'd done to ruin both of their lives, but she'd felt the need to protect him. And now, she and Angelina would be Bethany and Claire soon. A new life, a fresh start, shouldn't feel like such a death sentence. But it would be because they'd be living a life without Colin.

Head pounding, heart aching, she closed her eyes before leaning against the door and then sinking until her bottom hit the hardwood floor. She twisted off her wedding ring, noticing the red marks on her finger it left behind because it had always been a little too tight, and threw it across the room. Relief flooded her at getting that thing off her finger. She'd put it on so no one would question her about it. The only reason she'd held on to the ring was because she figured she could sell it if times got tight. The government had made promises to her, but who really knew if they could be trusted? They'd allowed Richard to slip through their fingers and that wasn't exactly reassuring.

Seconds turned into minutes and Melissa had no idea how long she'd been sitting there when she finally opened her eyes again.

Her father was safe. The baby was safe. Colin was safe. And she was exhausted.

She blocked out thoughts of how much Colin hated her now. She'd seen it in his eyes as he stalked toward her. The anger was so palpable that she'd had to turn her face away. Right then, she knew that he would never forgive her for leaving. And what had she really expected? For him to tell her everything would be okay? A hug?

Maybe it was good that Melissa Rancic would no longer exist in less than—she checked the clock—an hour. Maybe it was time to turn over a new leaf. Maybe it was time to make a new life for herself and Angelina. The thought of causing Colin any more pain was like a knife to her heart anyway. He deserved so much more.

She pushed up to stand as a knock sounded on the door from behind. She jumped. Her heart leapt to her throat and her chest squeezed. That same old feeling of panic, of the walls closing in and the air thinning, threatened to debilitate her. And that same question burned through her mind…had Richard found her?

No. That was impossible. He was probably in Canada by now.

The knocks sounded again, a little louder, a little more urgent.

Her mind spun. All the anxiety crashed down around her, freezing her limbs and making something as simple as taking a breath hurt.

Hold on a second. Richard wouldn't knock at her front door nor would anyone he sent.

That was way too direct. He would slip in during the night and slit her throat.

She glanced around the room, searching for a purse or jacket. Mrs. Klein most likely forgot something and she was returning to get it. The simple explanation was usually the right one no matter how much her brain protested and fear overtook her.

Melissa flipped the switch to the porch light and checked out the peephole. The light was out. Had it been like that before? Melissa couldn't remember. This was an old house. It belonged to her cousin's best friend. It had a lot of quirks.

Yes. It had. She remembered a little while ago when Mrs. Klein had gone home that the porch light hadn't been working. No way was Melissa opening that door without confirmation.

"Mrs. Klein?" Melissa said softly, and then waited for a response.

A high-pitched murmur of acknowledgment came.

As Melissa opened the door, she said, "What did you—"

And then froze.

She gasped as panic roared through her. She quickly regained her bearings and pushed the door, trying to shut it quickly even though it wouldn't budge. There was something wedged at the base. She glanced down. The toe of Colin's boot stared up at her.

"Not so fast, Melissa." He pushed open the door a little too easily and brushed past her.

"YOU SHOULDN'T BE HERE," Melissa said with more panic than anger, and he noticed that she'd positioned her body between him and the stairs. Was she blocking him for a reason? Was someone up there? Richard?

"I almost didn't come." Colin had followed Melissa on a whim. And then he'd sat at the end of the street trying to decide if he should knock or not. Seeing her with Richard would knife him, but maybe he needed that reinforcement to be able to finally let go. He'd been stuck in a place between still loving her and the kind of pain he wouldn't wish on his worst enemy for the past year. Seeing her dredged up feelings he thought he'd learned to live with, or live without, depending on how he looked at it.

"Why did you?" she asked.

"Is *he* here?" Colin motioned toward the base of the staircase, ignoring her question. That old anger from her leaving him for a flash-in-the-pan guy like Richard renewed.

She looked down and then shook her head. He didn't realize he'd been holding his breath until that moment. Forcing himself to exhale slowly, he also noticed that she wasn't wearing her ring anymore and she looked completely wrung out. Had the two of them been in a fight?

Colin shouldn't want to interfere with a married couple's business, but part of him needed to know that she was okay. "Did he do anything to you? Hurt you in any way?"

"No," she said quickly. He couldn't help but notice how her body was trembling.

He made a move toward her and she flinched. Another sign he didn't like.

"Why did you come to the ranch?" He pinned her with his stare, letting his anger show in his words. He couldn't afford to let her get inside his head or his heart.

"I wanted to see you," she said, looking like she'd had to force the words out. She didn't budge or invite him in, and she kept glancing toward the door like she expected her husband to walk through at any minute.

"Why?" he asked.

"We're moving out of the country and I guess I got nostalgic for the past." The corner of her mouth twitched. She was lying.

"Where are you going?" he asked.

She flashed her eyes at him but didn't speak.

Her body trembled as she brought her hand to her chest, signs that she was in a panic.

Nostalgia? This seemed an over-the-top reaction to being a little homesick.

"Everything going okay between the two of you?" Colin asked, a piece of him hoping she would say it wasn't. There was so much off about her, he noticed. From her reaction to him to the way she talked about her husband, Colin didn't know where to start with questions.

She nodded that it was. And that should be enough for Colin. He should walk right out the door and never look back. She'd broken his heart once, and this little visit was reopening old wounds that he had no doubt were going to sting for a long while after she left. If his heart was a muscle, it was memory causing his body to have this reaction to seeing her again, the one where he felt like the world was going to tumble down around him as soon as he walked out that door.

None of those feelings were welcomed. He stared at her, trying to read her to see if he could figure out why she'd really shown up at the ranch earlier. There was a time when knowing what was on her mind would've been second nature. But she'd changed. Colin might not be able to tell what she was thinking but he knew fear when he saw it. And she was afraid of something. If not her husband, then who? Him?

"So, he's treating you right?" he asked, unable to stop pushing for the answers he really wanted but his pride wouldn't allow him to ask. Like why she'd really ditched him for Richard in the first place.

"I said he was," she said, and her body language changed. She folded her arms and gritted her back teeth in the way that she did when she was shoring her strength.

"You're the one who came to see me and now you act like you can't stand to be in the same room," he said.

"Time for you to go," she shot back.

Was she there to torture him? To remind him of what he'd lost? Did she really hate him that much?

A piece of him had to know if she'd walked away because she'd really stopped loving him like she'd said. He stalked toward her and she walked backward until she was against the wall. The stairs were to the left and the hallway to the right would take him into the kitchen.

Melissa's hands came up in defense and she turned her face away, shutting her eyes.

This close, her heart thumped at the base of her throat wildly. The air changed and electricity pinged between them.

Their sexual chemistry hadn't dimmed. Were her feelings for him really dead?

"You're not getting away so easy this time." Colin used his thumb on her chin to guide her face toward him. His other hand wrapped around the base of her neck. Being this close took a toll on him, on his body. He took in a sharp breath and, by accident, breathed in her scent. At least one thing hadn't changed about her. She still smelled like sunshine after the first spring rain. All flowers and fresh air. "Why'd you take off your ring?"

She kept her eyes shut.

"I'm not leaving until you look at me and give me an answer." She'd never been able to do that and lie. A piece of him dared to hope she was done with her marriage, that she could admit it had been a mistake and that she'd never stopped loving him. Colin knew it was his bruised ego wishing for that. Because he had enough pride to realize that he would never love her in the same way again no matter what excuses she gave for walking out. That innocence had been shattered into a thousand tiny pieces along with his heart, and he doubted he could ever love anyone in that same way again, especially not her.

Melissa opened her eyes, slowly, and it was like the sun cresting on the horizon. Those violet streaks like rays, bathing darkness with light. His heart clenched and his muscles corded as her hands came up to his chest. He expected a jab or for her to push him away, but instead she double fisted his shirt and tugged him toward her.

All rationale flew out the window as Colin's pulse kicked up a few notches. He shouldn't want to dip down and claim her heart-shaped pink lips again. He shouldn't want to pull her body flush with his. He shouldn't want to get lost inside her.

And that's where he stopped.

Because he could never trust her enough to close his eyes again.

He pulled back, a little stunned at how easy it was to get trapped in old habits. How many times had they been in a similar position? Eager to rip each other's clothes off and let the feelings they had for each other consume them in a splendid, heated flame until they lay gasping for air, their arms and legs tangled. How easy it had been to talk to her, to laugh with her.

And look where that had gotten him. Rejected. Hurt.

Anger flooded him because she was messing with his mind and the future they would never have—a future he shouldn't want.

All he needed was to regain his sanity because Melissa was bad for him, and he knew that even if his body said otherwise.

She seemed to quickly regain her composure, and then she ducked out of his grasp.

"How did you know where to find me?" she asked.

"You weren't hard to follow speeding through town," he said.

"I have somewhere to be," she said. "You need to leave."

Colin glanced at his watch. "At eleven forty at night?"

"Yes," she said with too much conviction. She was either lying or hiding something.

"Seems late for an appointment," he said.

"I'm meeting up with someone...with *him*." Her face morphed for a split second like it did when she felt guilty.

"Why did you come back?" he asked.

"Doesn't matter. I'm not staying," she responded.

"Carolina said you wanted to talk to me," he pressed.

"She's mistaken."

He shot her a look.

"I'm the one who made a mistake. I shouldn't have gone to the ranch. Richard will be livid if he finds you here, so you need to go."

"Fine." Was she lying to protect Colin because he could see that she wasn't being truthful? There was no way to shield him now. Not after what she'd done to him. No one could convince him that she cared for his feelings.

"I didn't see your parents earlier. Would you tell them happy anniversary for me?" she asked, and he'd almost forgotten about that. They would have been married forty-two years next week.

But, wait, she hadn't heard the news? Sheriff Tommy Johnson had done a great job of keeping the murder investigation out of the papers, but Colin assumed that everyone knew his parents had died. He glanced down and back before shaking his head. He still had a hard time finding the right words to talk about it.

"What?" She searched his gaze as if what he was about to say would be stamped there.

"They're gone," he managed to say.

"Oh, no," she said with a little more alarm than seemed appropriate under the circumstances. She shouldn't care about him or his family anymore. "What happened?"

"Tommy's investigating their deaths," he said, and a curious look overtook her features. Sheriff Johnson was a close friend and grew up with all six of the O'Brien boys. He was more like family and was taking the murder investigation even more personally as a result of how much he cared for the O'Brien family. Colin couldn't pinpoint what was pinging through her thoughts but he could almost see the wheels churning. What was that all about?

"I'm so sorry," she said, and she looked stunned. Maybe a little guilty, too.

Colin had every intention of figuring out why.

"Are you telling me that you didn't know?" he asked, surprised, his curiosity getting the best of him.

"No." She shook her head as though for emphasis. Did she really hate him so much that she'd completely cut herself off from any news about Bluff? About his folks? She'd cared about them once. "How long have you been here?"

"Not long. This is just a quick stop on my way to—" she paused and he figured she was about to make something up. "Galveston." She raked her teeth across her bottom lip. "I'm so sorry about your parents."

She'd been especially close to his mother. His mom had made sure that Melissa was included in all their family celebrations, saying over and over that it was about time there was a little more estrogen at the table. Mom had said that after being surrounded by six boys—

boys that she adored—for most of her life that she couldn't wait to have a girl in the family.

For a minute, she looked shocked and a little frail, which was unlike Melissa. She must've figured out what he was thinking because her defenses flared. "I always cared about your parents, you know that. Especially your mother. I would've sent something if I'd realized."

Her voice broke and a look passed behind her eyes that he couldn't quite pinpoint when she said that last word.

Did she know something about the murders?

No. No way. She didn't even know his parents were gone before he told her.

Chapter Three

The only things keeping Melissa upright and on her feet were sheer determination and willpower. The second she'd heard the news about Colin's parents she'd almost buckled. Had her worst fears been realized? Had Richard gotten to them because of some sick need to punish her? So many other questions swirled. If Mr. O'Brien was having an affair, could that be connected to the murders? Melissa quieted her internal thoughts. It was dangerous to give away her reaction to the news. She couldn't risk Colin having any suspicion about Richard.

The news would spread soon enough that he was a criminal on the run, and Melissa would be long gone. Her handler, Marshal Davis, had been keeping the situation out of the news until Melissa could disappear. Speaking of which, it was almost time to meet him. If she didn't show at their rendezvous point, he'd start looking for her and she didn't need him asking around or giving more cause for concern. There were enough red flags in the air and she'd done enough damage on her own coming to Bluff.

An immediate problem of six feet two inches of raw masculinity stood in front of her. Melissa needed to think of a way to get him out of there so she could grab her sleeping infant and run. A wave of guilt assaulted her at thinking how much Colin had missed—how much he would miss—of his daughter's life. But with Richard on the loose, it was even more important to keep Colin and the baby separate for both of their protection.

If Colin knew about his daughter, it would be impossible to keep him away or stop him from fighting for custody. Once things settled down, the ranch would be an obvious place for Richard to look. As long as he was on the loose, Angelina was in danger.

But it was Colin's parents. She had to know if there was even a slight possibility that Richard could've been involved. "Like I said, I'm truly sorry to hear about your parents, Colin. When did it happen?"

"They were killed September of last year." His words were a sober reminder of how dangerous Richard could be. A thought struck.

Could she leave Angelina with Colin? The ranch was probably safer than the US Treasury.

No. It wouldn't work. Richard believed Angelina was his daughter. If he heard or saw her with Colin it would be too easy to put the pieces together. Until Richard was safely locked away or dead, she couldn't risk it. She mumbled an apology under her breath and a prayer for forgiveness.

"What happened to them?" she asked.

"At first, we believed Dad had a heart attack while driving and wrecked with both him and Mom in the car. Something felt off to Tommy so he ran labs. Toxicology report came back with poison in their systems," he said.

"That's awful. How on earth could they be poisoned?" Melissa's heart broke at hearing the details.

"Tommy doesn't know. It would have to be someone who had access to both of them. Mom had hosted their annual party for local artists earlier that night, so a few people had admission to the ranch," he said.

"I'm guessing Tommy already checked everyone out at the party, including staff," she said, still trying to absorb the news. It was selfish to think about the fact that Angelina would never know her grandparents. There was always some small part of Melissa wishing things would magically work out and she and Colin would end up together. It was a crazy notion that had given her the tiniest sliver of hope in what had been the worst year of her life save for the birth of her child.

"He did. All he has so far is the poison. He doesn't know how it got in their systems or what the motive for murder could be," Colin said. "There's a slight chance that they ingested the poison accidentally."

"Except what are the chances they both ingested the same thing at the same time?" she said out loud, not meaning to. She shouldn't add fuel to the fire. Colin might find out the truth about his father and that would crush him. She still could scarcely believe that the man would have an affair. She'd argued with Richard, putting up more of a fight than she knew better to, refusing to accept his accusation at first. And that had led to an even bigger fight between them when he'd accused her of defending the O'Briens because she still loved Colin.

In order to survive, she'd had to swallow her emotions and convince Richard that she loved him. Only him. If someone had told her that she'd be able to sell that lie a year ago she would've laughed. Finding out she was pregnant had changed her priorities.

Nothing mattered more to her than keeping Colin's baby safe.

As a mother, she'd found a new well of strength to draw from than she had ever known existed inside her. Angelina's safety took precedence over everyone and everything.

"It's late, Colin. I need to go," she said, using all the courage she could muster to speak those words. Being with Colin again was taking a toll on her, body, soul and mind. She was grateful that Angelina was a sound sleeper. Melissa had a prayer of getting out of this situation without doing any more damage.

Coming back to Bluff had been a mistake. Seeing the pain in Colin's eyes was heartbreaking. And that would be the last image she would have of him to hold on to. She had hoped to see him happy, to see his charismatic smile. His sexy half grin that had been so good at making her pulse race and her body ache in that perfect way. She hadn't counted on seeing him still so miserable. Or wanting to touch him so much that she physically hurt.

Blocking out the pain, an act she'd mastered in the past twelve months, she pushed past him and then opened the front door wide. She needed to meet her handler so she could disappear. The thought she was running from her problems struck. She pushed it aside.

Yes, the man standing in front of her was an issue. Yes, he deserved to know about Angelina. Yes, his daughter deserved to know about him. Not now. Not if it meant putting their little girl in danger. Even Colin would agree that Angelina had to come first.

She pushed the door open as wide as it would go.

"Please, Colin, don't make me ask again." She prayed he didn't pick up on the desperate note in her tone.

COLIN SAT IN his vehicle contemplating the conversation he'd just had with Melissa for a good twenty minutes. Something about the way she'd asked him to leave didn't sit right. Forget the electricity they still shared, sex had always been a whole other experience with her, and it was muscle memory causing the heat between them to sizzle like it was yesterday. He'd felt the chemistry, loud and powerful, when her back had been against the wall and there wasn't more than a foot of space between her full breasts and his chest.

She was married to someone else and Colin would never act on his impulses. He'd stopped having sex for sex's sake when he became old enough to fight for his country. He'd done a tour and then returned home. His reputation for dating around might be true, but he was selective when it came to who he spent time with and even more so with women he slept with.

Colin had an ironclad commandment about not messing around with another man's wife. Even if he and Melissa had belonged to each other at one time, his rule was etched in stone and applied no matter how much his heart tried to protest. Or tell him that she was still his after all this time.

Logic ruled. It was time to move on.

Then there was the reaction she'd had to the news about his parents and the questions that had followed.

What was the point of worrying about it? She'd said that she was about to move and was homesick. Colin needed to accept it and move on. He was just about to start his ignition and drive off when he saw twin headlights exit the alley. Curiosity got the best of him, so he followed Melissa's car. All he needed was to see her with Richard to imprint the new reality of her being married to someone else into his brain. Colin was visual and he needed that image in order to stamp out all those other thoughts that kept creeping in. Thoughts of how sweet she still smelled, all floral and sunshine. Thoughts of how soft her skin still was when he'd touched her arm. Thoughts of how rapid her breathing had become when they were standing too close. All of which was dangerous for Colin to acknowledge.

Melissa was married to Richard Rancic. The words sat bitter on his tongue as he cut right, allowing enough distance between cars so that she wouldn't realize she was being followed. She'd made her choice. She was Melissa Rancic now. It was high time his mind caught up.

Cutting right a few seconds after she did, he was flooded with memories—memories he fought to keep from overtaking his thoughts. Letting go of her wasn't going to be easy but he'd find a way. He had to. Because a little voice, the one that still knew her, said that once she left town she wasn't coming back this time. Colin's heart fisted again. He reminded himself that it was a good thing to acknowledge and accept the situation for what it was.

Melissa made another turn into the parking lot of the lawnmower store at the edge of town. It was located at the edge of the last neighborhood in Bluff before hay bales and country roads dotted the landscape. The lots were one-to-two acres in this area.

On three sides of the parking lot were woods, basically mesquite trees with two feet of underbrush. It was most likely Colin's military training that had him checking the perimeter for any signs of danger and not the hairs that pricked on the back of his neck. Why would she meet her husband after midnight in an empty parking lot?

Scenarios started running through his mind as he pulled past the lot, turned off his headlights and then made a U-turn. Was it his heart and not his logical mind saying that she wanted out of the marriage? If there had been abuse she would be smarter to meet out in the open in a busy place, like a restaurant. This would be the worst possible spot. Empty, abandoned for all practical purposes. Images of her being abducted against her will assaulted him. And that was most likely his training taking over. Now he really needed to stick around to make sure she was okay.

There was a street lamp in the middle of the empty parking lot, and that was the only light around. The building was completely blacked out. All of Colin's danger radar flared. He wanted her to park under the light at least.

She didn't.

Melissa parked at the far corner of the lot with woods to each side. What was she thinking? He thought he'd trained her better than that in personal safety in the time they were together. She might be meeting her husband but any whacko could take advantage of this situation.

Did she really not have sense enough to think this through? Or had he rattled her? He blamed himself for that, figuring their conversation had upset her more than she'd wanted to let on. Seeing her again had certainly done a number on him.

Colin pulled over to the side of the road where he could see vehicles as they entered and exited the lot. There was only one other place a car could turn in and it came from a country road that ended at Sander's farm a half hour down the road.

He wanted eyes on Rancic. And then he could finally convince himself to let her go.

A light blue sedan turned right into the lot fifteen minutes later. Colin exited his vehicle and moved stealthily along the tree line in order to get a good look at the exchange, telling himself that he needed to be close enough to see their faces. Maybe he was a glutton for punishment, and it seemed his heart would agree with that statement as a knifelike pain stabbed through him with each forward step. He told himself that he was making ground on being able to let go of the grip she had on him, still had on him. That thought carried his steps forward.

The headlights illuminated Melissa's car and Colin could see her clearly from his position as she exited her vehicle. She should be happy to see her husband, shouldn't she?

All Colin saw clearly was fear as Rancic parked and cut the lights. Colin moved to get a better look. Melissa's attention shifted from Rancic to the backseat of her car as she backed away from him.

What was that all about?

Colin's fear that their marriage had gone sour seemed to be playing out in front of him. Based on her expression, she was scared to death of the guy.

All his instincts told him to walk away. Melissa had made her choice and it wasn't his place to interfere with a husband and wife. And yet he knew without a doubt that he was about to do just that…interfere. She could thank him or curse him later.

As Colin broke out of the tree line, the sheriff's cruiser sped across the lot. Melissa used the distraction to lock herself inside the vehicle. Smart. He'd hang back behind her car and let Tommy do his job.

Rancic dove into his vehicle and managed to come up behind the wheel. He gunned the engine in reverse, burning rubber. His tires finally gripped the concrete and he sped backward.

Tommy must not've seen the barrel of the

shotgun poking out from the driver's side an inch or two as he hit his brakes, no doubt ready to turn around and give chase. Fire shot out the end as the blast split the air, burning through Colin's ears as he pushed off the back of Melissa's vehicle and bolted toward the sheriff's SUV.

Rancic was out of there by the time Colin reached Tommy.

He pulled his friend from his vehicle and laid him out on the cement. Blood was everywhere as Colin scanned Tommy's body, assessing the damage.

"Damn shotgun," Tommy said, and his voice was a little too calm. No doubt, he was in shock.

Colin knew enough about weapons to know just how dangerous shotgun shells were to bulletproof vests. They weren't rated for those because they didn't have a consistent velocity. Tommy had taken a bullet to his left side and blood covered his shirt. A red dot flowered. Colin needed to stop the bleeding.

"How bad is it? Be honest," Tommy said as he searched Colin's face, no doubt looking for a reaction so he could gauge his injury.

"You're going to be just fine." It was the lie every soldier had told no matter how grave the damage looked.

He maintained his game face and could only pray that no major organs or arteries had been pierced as he shrugged out of his T-shirt and then used it to place pressure on the wound.

Suddenly Melissa was there, too, and sounds of a baby crying came from a distance.

"It's getting colder out here," Tommy said, already shivering.

"Stay with me, man," Colin said.

"What can I do?" Melissa asked as Colin looked up at her.

"Call 911. *Now*," he said.

Chapter Four

Colin paced in Bluff General's waiting room after giving his statement to Deputy Garcia. The deputy had gone to speak to hospital staff, leaving Colin to wait alone for updates.

Blue carpet, blue chairs and stark white walls couldn't erase the bloody images scrolling through Colin's mind. There was blood on his shirt, Tommy's blood. Tommy had been shot by Melissa's husband. *Estranged husband*, a little voice in his head clarified. Colin could hardly wrap his thoughts around what had happened even though he'd seen it with his own eyes.

Tommy had been immediately taken into surgery, and Colin had called his brothers to deliver the news. His eldest brother, Dallas, was on his way to the hospital. The others would soon follow. Tommy needed all the family around him that he could get, and the O'Briens were a tight-knit bunch.

Personally, Colin had seen the inside of the county hospital a few too many times recently. As far as desirable places to end up went, Bluff General bottomed his list. In the six months since his parents' murders, several of his brothers had ended up in a room not unlike the one Tommy was in now. Many of his siblings had also found the loves of their lives in recent months, but that was a whole different subject. Colin had believed that he'd found his in Melissa.

If that weren't enough to make his head spin, Melissa had a baby. Colin didn't want to acknowledge the anger burning through his chest, considering she'd been adamant about waiting to have children with him.

He forced himself to stop pacing and take a seat.

The thought of Melissa having Richard Rancic's child hit Colin harder than a battering ram. It made her marriage to another man feel very real. Thinking back to the way she'd acted so cagey at the house and how quickly she'd ushered him out the door had him wondering if she'd wanted to hide her baby from him. Richard Rancic was a criminal and a jerk. For the life of Colin he couldn't figure out why she'd marry the guy, let alone have his child. Colin stabbed his fingers through his dark hair. Speaking of Melissa, she should be there by now. He glanced around.

Dallas should arrive any minute. Tommy was more like a brother than a friend and he was fighting for his life. Going over the scenario again and again was about to make Colin's head explode.

Caffeine. He needed a giant cup of black coffee about now.

Colin pushed off the chair as Melissa rounded the corner. A pink blanket swathed a small bundle cradled in her arms. Melissa's baby was somehow tinier than he'd expected. The child must be asleep because she didn't move.

"How's Tommy?" Melissa's eyes were wide and stress lines bracketed her mouth. She glanced down at her baby and another emotion flickered that he had trouble pinpointing. Guilt?

"He's in surgery," Colin said, noticing how she kept one arm underneath the little bundle and her other hand on the baby's back. How much did it blow his mind to think that Melissa had a daughter?

Damn.

"What happened back there? You told me that you were meeting your husband and then you looked scared to death when he showed. What aren't you telling me?" Colin asked, taking note of the dark look that passed behind her eyes when he said the word *husband*.

"It's nothing. A misunderstanding," Melissa said, and the corner of her mouth twitched in the way it did when she was scared.

"That's impossible. Tommy's lying on a bed being cut open right now and that sure isn't because of nothing," Colin said, his voice raised in frustration.

"I didn't mean—" The little girl stirred and panic washed over Melissa's features.

He needed to take a minute to calm down.

"I can't talk about it right now," she said quietly, motioning toward the baby.

Colin rubbed his chin and turned to face the other direction. He couldn't help but notice how natural Melissa looked holding her daughter and he shouldn't want the child in her arms to be his. She wasn't. That reality crashed around Colin like a rogue wave, unexpected and all-consuming. It caught him off guard, but he couldn't afford to care right now. Not with Tommy down the hall in surgery and Melissa tight-lipping his questions about her husband.

Part of his anger had to do with his pent-up emotions about Melissa. He'd have to figure out a way to make peace with the fact that she'd married someone else and was now a mother. The thought was going to take a minute to sink in. Seeing the little girl made good strides toward acceptance.

"Have you been happy?" He surprised himself with the question.

"About her?" she asked, and then answered before he could respond. "Absolutely."

There was so much conviction in her voice that he didn't question her answer.

"What was all that about back there, Melissa? I saw Richard. I know he shot Tommy," he said. Her husband's name sat bitterly on his tongue. "What's he doing that you won't talk about?"

She turned away from him.

"The man just shot a sheriff, Melissa," Colin said, his anger on the rise again. He shouldn't be frustrated at thinking about a time when there were no secrets between them. She'd betrayed him, he reminded himself, needing to gain his bearings again. Because his heart stirred while standing this close to her, and he didn't want to care this much about anyone ever again. He told himself that his reaction had to do more with her safety than his own out-of-control emotions.

Melissa bounced her little girl gently, continuing to ignore him while the baby slept. Curiosity was starting to get the best of him. He couldn't see the baby's face, which was just a distraction anyway, and he wasn't sure he could handle seeing the product of Richard and Melissa together. More proof that Melissa had never belonged to him in the first place. Then again, maybe that's exactly what he needed: a reality check.

"I can't talk about it with you," she said.

"Can't or won't?"

"Does it matter? Either way I'm not talking, Colin." Again, hearing his name on her tongue brought an onslaught of feelings he needed to ignore.

"Why not, Melissa?" Did she hate him that much?

"It's complicated," she said on a sigh, still bouncing as the nervous tick returned.

On closer look, there was so much stress and worry in her eyes.

"What's going on between you and your husband?" Colin asked a little too loudly, causing the baby to stir again.

"Shhh. You'll wake her." Melissa patted the little girl's back and started humming.

Colin didn't want to disturb the baby. From what he knew about little ones, which wasn't much until recently, once they were awake all grown-up discussion ceased.

Maybe he needed a minute to clear his thoughts. His emotions were riding high after watching one of his best friends take a bullet. Seeing Melissa at the ranch earlier had sent him to a dark place to begin with, and watching her now wasn't improving the situation.

"I need coffee," he said, stalking out the door, needing to walk away and gain some perspective. He didn't want to notice how much she was trembling or how hard she was working to put on a brave front. Her eyes had always been her tell, and right now hers said that she was terrified. Of Colin? No way could she think he would hurt her. Her husband was another story and one Colin planned to hear in detail before he let her walk out that door again. And especially now that Richard had tried to kill a sheriff.

The coffee was just how Colin liked it, strong and hot. He took a sip to clear his head. Took another when that didn't work. There were too many residual feelings coloring his thoughts, not to mention the stress that came with not knowing how Tommy was doing yet. Colin had already checked three times in fifteen minutes before Melissa had arrived.

"Any word on Tommy?" Dallas asked as he walked inside the break room.

"All I know is that he's in surgery." Colin gave his brother a bear hug before shaking his head. He poured a fresh cup and then handed it to Dallas. "It could be a while before we hear anything."

"Well then, no news is probably good news." Dallas took a sip, worry lines etched in his forehead as he gave Colin a once-over, his gaze fixed on the large red stain centered on Colin's shirt.

"It's all his blood. I'm fine," Colin reassured.

"I might have an extra shirt in my truck if you want to put on something clean," Dallas offered.

Colin had washed his hands not long after arriving at the hospital when a nurse had tried to put him in a wheelchair and take him into the back for a check. He'd had to lift his shirt to show her there were no marks on his body to convince her.

"I may take you up on that," he said to Dallas.

"You said Tommy was in the parking lot of Zahn Lawn Mower Supply. Any idea what he was doing out there so late?" Dallas asked. Colin had only given his brother essential information. Tommy had been shot and he was at Bluff General. Richard Rancic was armed and dangerous.

"Good question." There was another one that would follow.

"What were you doing there?" Dallas didn't wait long to hit him with that one. That was an even better question. Colin was still trying to figure that out. Dallas didn't ask about Melissa, but the questions about her were written in his tense expression.

"She ran away so fast at the Fling," he finally said.

Dallas compressed his lips and gave a nod, saying he understood. It was good that someone did because Colin was still scratching his head over the night's events. Talk about an evening going haywire. His friend was fighting for his life in a hospital bed and the woman he'd wanted to marry had a child.

"What did she say when you showed up?" Dallas asked.

"I parked to the side, trying to decide if I was going to talk to her or not." It wasn't entirely untrue. "Then, I saw her husband pull into the lot and she seemed real uncomfortable. I thought she was supposed to be meeting him." Colin's voice hitched on that last word.

"Why would a husband be meeting his wife

in a parking lot at midnight?" Dallas asked, and then sipped his coffee.

"I'd like to hear the answer to that question for myself, but she's not talking." Based on her terrorized expression when she saw Richard, he was the last person she'd expected to show. It was clear to Colin that she was scared to death of the guy, which made even less sense. Rancic was a jerk and his business reputation said he was cutthroat. Didn't make him a criminal. So, why did the guy show up and then shoot a sheriff? Obviously, there was a lot going on. Had Melissa left her husband? Was Richard so determined to get her back that he'd shot a sheriff, realized what he'd done and then fled the scene?

"So, she's here?" Dallas asked.

Colin nodded.

"Have you spoken to her?" Dallas's eyebrow shot up.

"There hasn't been much time. She stayed back with officers at the scene. I've been busy giving all the information I could to the hospital workers since I was the one who'd been stemming the blood flow and administering CPR. And then I gave a statement to the deputy," Colin said.

"Garcia?" Dallas asked.

Colin nodded again.

"Melissa just showed up here a few minutes ago and it didn't exactly go well between us," he said with a shrug. "Guess I needed a minute to clear my head before taking another go at it with her."

"It's hard when you have so much history," Dallas agreed.

When Colin had been standing close to her at the house, he hadn't noticed anything unusual on her body. There was no bruising, no other marks of any kind indicating abuse. She still had that same rosy skin, a combination of cream and silk. And yet she was terrified of her husband and that made Colin believe their relationship had been abusive.

"She has a kid now," was all Colin said. He took a sip of coffee.

"You okay?" Dallas asked. "I can take things from here if you want to go cool off somewhere. Go get cleaned up and come back."

"I'll be fine. Me and Melissa were a long time ago," he said, mostly for his own benefit. "A lot's changed since we went out, and let's not forget that she's married to someone else."

Dallas did the "tight lip/nod" thing again. "That's probably a healthy way to look at it."

"Not much choice, is there." It wasn't a question. He didn't repeat the fact that she and Richard had a child together. Colin could've lived the rest of his life without knowing that detail.

Dallas shrugged with an apologetic look.

"Here's what else I know. Tommy comes roaring through the parking lot soon after Rancic, no lights or sirens. And then I'm really confused about what's going on," Colin continued. "The next thing I see is Tommy being shot. Rancic squeals out of the parking lot and I'm trying to save my friend's life."

"That's a lot to have coming at you at once." Dallas shot a look that said he was talking about more than the incident in the parking lot with Tommy.

Colin studied his coffee cup before taking a sip.

"For the record, I still think it's a good idea to get some fresh air," Dallas added.

"I'm not leaving until I know Tommy's going to be okay and I get a few answers out of Melissa. Who knows when she'll take off and I might never see her again." Colin ground his back teeth. He gripped the coffee cup a little too tight.

"You sure about that last part?" Dallas's brow lifted.

"As sure as the sun rises in the east," Colin said.

Another one of Dallas's concerned looks creased his brother's forehead.

"It might help that you're here. She always liked you and she never did anything to put a wedge between the two of you," Colin said.

"Hell yes she did," Dallas said without hesitation. "She hurt my brother."

Colin topped off both of their cups before urging his brother out of the lounge. "Let's go get some answers."

MELISSA TEXTED HER handler for the sixth time since the incident in the parking lot and an ominous feeling settled over her. Where was Marshal Davis? And how on earth had Richard found her? He was supposed to be in Canada by now. If Tommy and Colin hadn't shown when they did she'd be dead.

Her body trembled no matter how hard she tried to settle down. A thought struck. Was there any possibility that Richard was the reason Marshal Davis hadn't shown?

The US marshal was most likely a victim of Bluff's spotty cell coverage, but being without contact after everything that had happened caused a cold chill to trickle down her spine. That uneasy feeling gripped her again as she rocked Angelina.

Tommy Johnson was shot and she couldn't help but blame herself. If she had stayed away from Bluff none of this would be happening.

Her stress levels were climbing through the roof and another big part of that had to do with the man down the hall. Colin would be back any second with questions she couldn't answer. And especially not without speaking to Marshal Davis first.

Angelina whimpered in her sleep.

"It's okay, sweet girl," Melissa soothed, wishing it were that simple in all areas of her life.

Thinking about the possibility of Colin realizing the little girl was his daughter sent another tremor racing through Melissa. She couldn't allow him to put the pieces together, to know about Angelina. She'd done a great job of hiding the little girl's face so far. Could she keep it up until Marshal Davis showed? He *had* to show. He was her ticket to a new life, a safe life.

Melissa needed to get out of Bluff and disappear. Witness protection never sounded better. Although, there was no way she could leave without knowing Tommy was going to be okay. And she didn't dare risk Angelina's life by walking out the hospital door alone. Melissa was no fool. Richard was out there, somewhere. He would make good on his promise to destroy her and everyone she loved if he saw her.

Suddenly, the walls felt like they were closing in because if Colin figured out that Angelina was his, there'd be no walking out that door without him.

Okay, breathe.

The world seemed like it was crumbling down around her. All she had to do was let her baby sleep while Melissa obstructed the view of her face until her handler called. She could do that. She'd been through so much more in the past year. Melissa wanted to run, to escape in her car and disappear. She wasn't fool enough to go outside without protection.

Richard had nothing to lose. He was already wanted by the federal government. And now, a sheriff who happened to be her childhood friend lay on an operating table because of Richard—*because of her*. Icy tendrils gripped her spine as her pulse raced. She checked her cell's screen again. No messages.

Melissa stood up and then crossed the waiting room. Maybe she could find another place to sit and still be safe? On second thought, she seriously doubted it. The hospital had security but not the caliber she needed to keep Richard at bay. There was no place to hide from him except here with the O'Briens, where Colin could protect her and Angelina.

A panicked feeling made Melissa pace even

faster. Everything inside her wanted to run out that door and keep going, except her heart. That stubborn organ wanted to be near Colin because he was the only person who'd ever made her feel safe. She'd taken that for granted when they'd been together before. But then, what had she had to run from? She'd had no idea what kind of monster lurked in Bluff a year ago. Any creature that she could conjure in her mind paled in comparison to Richard. He was worse than a monster. He was pure evil.

The scuffle of boots sounded in the hallway and she didn't need to turn around to know that Colin had entered the room. She faced him.

"Dallas," she said, startled. In an attempt to recover, she added, "It's good to see you again."

"You, too, Melissa." Dallas stood behind his brother.

Melissa hoped he couldn't hear her heart thudding against her ribs at the thought of two O'Briens in the room. If either one of them got a look at her daughter it was over.

It wasn't a selfish desire that had her wanting to keep Angelina a secret. Although she had that, too. It was survival. Either of them figured out paternity and Colin would follow her to the ends of the earth to find her and his child. But then, she hadn't really thought this through because this whole room would be filled with O'Briens soon.

Her chest squeezed thinking about it. She was trying to move away from danger, not put everyone in front of the firing squad. As long as Angelina was resting, Melissa should be able to hide her true identity. *Sleep, my little angel. Sleep.*

Melissa couldn't allow herself to think about anything but Tommy being okay. Finding her handler ran a close second.

"I take it no one's come in with an update?" Dallas asked as Colin moved by the window and stared outside.

She desperately wanted to ask him to move away from there.

"Not yet," she said. "I'm really sorry about what happened to Tommy."

A few tears free-fell despite her attempts to force them back.

"It's not your fault," Colin said under his breath.

She wasn't so sure.

"I can help you with your daughter if you'd like a break," Dallas said, offering to hold her.

"No," Melissa said too quickly. "I just don't want to take a chance of waking her with everything going on."

The blanket slipped with movement and she secured it back in place. With Dallas standing close and Colin on the other side of the room, it was going to be a challenge to keep Angelina's face concealed.

Dallas's right brow raised but he didn't immediately comment.

"I never knew how little sleep any of our parents must've gotten until my son, Jackson, came into my life," he finally said, and then motioned toward chairs near Colin. "At least sit down."

"You have a child?" she asked as she glanced at the chairs and then at Colin. Angelina stirred and Melissa's heart dropped. *Please, little angel.*

"And a wife," Dallas said.

"What?" Melissa didn't mean to sound so shocked. She smiled at him as she moved to the farthest wall and took a seat.

"A lot has changed since you left," Dallas said with a glance toward Colin.

"Well, congratulations," she said. "You looked very happy when you mentioned your family."

Dallas smiled and took a seat next to her.

"What's her name?" He motioned toward the baby.

"Angelina," she said quietly. Out of her periphery, she saw Colin's reaction as his entire body tensed. It had been a moment of weakness that had her needing to use that name—the name that she and Colin had said they'd use if they ever had a daughter.

Dallas seemed to pick up on the added tension when he changed the subject by asking if Melissa wanted anything to drink.

"No, thanks," she said. "I'm still shocked at hearing you got married. It's good. And I think it's amazing that you have a son."

"It's funny how everyone tells you that you won't sleep when you have a baby, but no one says that you won't mind," Dallas said, that O'Brien pride written all over his features.

"I couldn't be happier for you, Dallas." She would bet any one of the O'Brien boys would make a great father, and her heart especially believed that about Colin. A wave of sadness crashed into her. She checked her phone again. The sooner she heard from Marshal Davis, the faster she could leave.

"Thank you. He's a great kid. I hope you'll swing by the ranch and meet my wife, Kate," he said, and that comment netted a harsh look from Colin.

"I'd like that," she said, even though the words were hollow. Liking the idea wasn't the problem. She'd be Bethany soon enough and would never be allowed to look back. And especially not while Richard was a free man. Probably not after, either, considering he managed a network of ruthless criminals.

Speaking of the devil, she really needed to update Marshal Davis about Richard being in Bluff. She hoped Davis wasn't waiting at their meet-up, but how could he be? She hadn't thought about it before but there'd been cell coverage in the parking lot. She'd used her phone to call for an ambulance and yet she hadn't heard from her handler.

Her cell buzzed, causing her to jump. She checked the text. Relief washed over her and through her when she saw the initials from her handler along with a text message. The second blessing was that Angelina didn't wake.

New meet-up location: Bluff Motel.

"I have to go." Melissa dropped the phone into her bag and felt around for the car keys.

Colin moved in between her and the door.

"You're not leaving without explaining yourself."

Chapter Five

The baby stirred at Colin's booming voice. Melissa's heart dropped. This time, Angelina whined and Melissa knew that her daughter was about to cry.

"Shhh, baby. It's okay," Melissa soothed. She needed to get out of there fast before Colin saw her daughter's face—correction, *their* daughter's face. All Melissa's plans at keeping everyone safe while starting a new life were being threatened. O'Brien men were too honest and too much about family for Colin to stand by while she took his daughter on the run without him knowing where they'd gone or if they'd return. Coming to the hospital had been a huge risk, but what choice did she have? She'd had no idea where her handler was and her daughter needed protection. The storm that had been brewing inside her was developing, swirling, threatening to devastate her.

There was a ray of sunshine, though. Marshal Davis had finally contacted her. He was okay. Melissa needed to get to the checkpoint so she could disappear. Wow, she didn't expect that word to hurt so much.

"I'll give you some privacy," Dallas said. He stopped as he rounded by Angelina and all Melissa could think was, *Keep walking, Dallas.*

Melissa feared he'd have questions, especially if he made a quick calculation and estimated Angelina's age. Her heart dropped as one of her worst nightmares threatened to play out before her eyes. She held her breath, waiting. Dallas gave her a look as he passed by but he didn't say a word.

She let out the breath she'd been holding.

"What's going on?" Colin's tone was harsh, his words like daggers being thrown at her.

"Colin, I can't do this right now," she shot back under her breath, trying to will her body to stop shaking. "I need to take care of my daughter and I have to go."

"Not until you tell me where," he said, and his athletic frame blocked the exit. "And not until I know you'll be safe."

"Richard is in trouble with the law and I'm going to meet with a US marshal. Everything will be fine," she said, her voice breaking on the last few words. Everything wasn't going to be fine. It hadn't been fine in a very long time. And Melissa feared that it would never be fine again.

"What has he done?" he asked.

"I can't talk about it. I told you what you wanted to know. Move out of the way," she said. Angelina took in a deep breath.

Colin folded his arms across his chest. "Not good enough, Melissa."

"Don't do this, Colin. I have to go. He's waiting for me," she said, and then it seemed to dawn on him why she'd be meeting with a US marshal.

At the same time, Angelina popped her head up and the blanket dipped. Melissa covered her as her daughter tried to follow the new voice…

Every muscle in Colin's body seemed to harden as shock and disbelief formed brackets around his mouth and creased his forehead. Did he know?

"Melissa…" was all he seemed able to get out as Angelina belted out the saddest-sounding cry.

"I can't right now," was all she said as she started pacing and soothing her daughter. Colin figuring out that Angelina was his daughter would cause all kinds of wrinkles in Melissa's plans. He'd turn the world over to find them if he allowed her outside that door in the first place.

Melissa's legs felt like rubber as her carefully constructed world crumbled around her. She was going to have to tell him at some point. *Not now*, a little voice said.

"Richard is armed and dangerous. There's no telling where he is, and I can't let you walk out that door if I don't know you're going to be protected. Period," Colin said.

"He's not going to hurt us," she countered, but there was no life in those words. She might be feeling defeated at the moment, but her determination would kick in soon and she'd recover. She'd get her life back on track. Richard did not get to win.

"What if you take us to the meet-up point?" she asked. Before she could answer Dallas stepped into the room with a man in uniform behind him. She recognized Deputy Garcia.

Angelina had settled on Melissa's shoulder again, and if Colin realized he had a daughter he didn't show it.

"Deputy Garcia has news that I think you need to hear," Dallas said.

After perfunctory greetings, the deputy said, "A US marshal was found shot on Highway 287. He was pronounced dead at the scene."

The air *whooshed* from Melissa's lungs and

she was almost knocked back a step. This couldn't be happening. This couldn't be real.

"When?" she asked, her knees buckling.

Colin caught her before she went down and helped her over to a nearby blue chair.

"His distress call came in just before midnight. Tommy had received a call for aid and he was following the gunman when he was shot," Deputy Garcia said, his voice anguished.

"Midnight?" she repeated, her voice trailing off. *How could that be?* She blinked up at Garcia. "This can't be real. You must be mistaken. He just texted me. He has to be alive."

"It couldn't have been him," Colin said, his gaze intense on her. He redirected, looking at Garcia instead. "Was the marshal's phone at the scene when they found him?"

"Hold on while I check." Garcia excused himself to make the call.

"If Marshal Davis didn't text me, who did?" Melissa asked, too stunned to accept that the marshal might be dead. He had a wife, kids. He couldn't be gone.

Garcia returned a few minutes later. "We don't know where his phone is. It's missing along with his laptop and the weapons in his trunk."

Richard had shot Marshal Davis. Richard had shot Tommy. And he'd shoot Melissa if he had a chance. Her only question was why he hadn't fired on her in the parking lot.

He didn't want to risk killing his daughter, a little voice in the back of her head said. She glanced down at her angel—the child that Richard believed to be his. Melissa couldn't even think that anything could happen to her.

"There's more. I just learned that the suspect's vehicle was last seen in this area. I need to take you into protective custody," Garcia said to her.

She was already shaking her head. If a US marshal couldn't keep her safe, how could Garcia? He didn't have half the resources available to him that the federal government would.

"I have to get her out of here," Colin said with a glance toward her. She could tell by his expression that he was expecting some kind of acknowledgment or agreement.

She was still too shocked to react.

"How do you plan to do that?" Garcia said. "I have a US marshal supervisor waiting to hear from me that she's okay and on her way in."

"They can't guarantee her safety. I can," Colin said emphatically.

"If we can get her to the ranch we should be okay," Dallas offered.

Colin was already shaking his head again.

"We're going off the grid. I don't want anyone to know where I take her," he said to Dallas. "Not even you guys."

"Can I refuse protective custody?" Melissa asked. So far, her handler was dead and her childhood friend was fighting for his life in surgery down the hallway.

Richard had followed and then shot a US marshal in order to find her. He'd stop at nothing and allow no one to step in his path because at this point he had nothing to lose.

The way she saw it, Colin was her best chance to survive, especially when he figured out that Angelina was his child. And he would figure it out soon at this rate.

Garcia nodded. "I can't advise that, though."

She looked to Colin. "Can you keep me and my daughter alive until they locate Richard and lock him away?"

She didn't even want to think about his brother or the others working in the organization who could come after her. Right now, she focused on Richard.

"He won't hurt either one of you on my watch." His words, steady as steel, carried a vow, a promise, and Colin had always delivered on his word.

"Then, I'm refusing your offer for protective custody," she said to Garcia. All Melissa cared about was keeping Angelina alive at this point. Nothing mattered more to her than her daughter and she couldn't even fathom anything happening to her little angel. There was no worse thought for a parent than losing a child. It was unfair, unthinkable and no one deserved it.

"We'll get farther if Dallas takes your daughter to the ranch and keeps her there while we go on the run," Colin said to her. His word choice made her realize that he hadn't figured it out yet.

"No way. She goes with me or no deal," Melissa said, holding on to her baby a little bit tighter to her chest.

"Listen, if we lead Richard away from here she'll be safer," Colin said, but there was no conviction in his words. He knew her well enough to know that this would be a losing battle. Colin had never been one to waste energy on lost causes and he'd see the threat to her by now.

"We'll send Fisher with you." Dallas also seemed to understand that leaving her baby behind wasn't an option. He was referring to Gideon Fisher, head of security at the ranch.

"No extra protection. We're more nimble if it's just us." Colin pulled his cell from his pocket and then handed it to his brother. "And no cell phones. I don't want to take a chance of anyone being able to locate us using the GPS in those."

He indicated that Melissa should do the same. She fished hers out of her handbag and stared at it. She'd become so dependent on her phone that the thought of handing it over—especially with so many other unknowns in her situation—brought on a wave of anxiety. But Angelina's life was on the line.

Melissa passed her phone over, her connection to the new life she was supposed to be making. Instead, she was going on the run. Life changes were like stray lightning. She never knew when a bolt was coming that could change her life forever. She'd learned not to depend on making plans in the past twelve months.

Right there, she made a silent vow not to rest until Richard was locked behind bars where he belonged. Angelina didn't deserve this life. And Melissa was prepared to do whatever it took in order to make sure her daughter never had to suffer because of that man again.

COLIN ONLY GOT a glimpse of the little girl's face and yet that one second had frozen the blood in his veins. There was no way that little girl could be his. Period. And this wasn't the time to discuss it. Although, he planned to have a conversation with Melissa as soon as he could allow himself to think about something besides Tommy healing and stopping Richard. For now, everything else was on hold.

The look on Melissa's face when Colin had asked her to let Dallas take her daughter was an image he wouldn't soon be able to erase. She'd been mother bear and desperate and heartbroken all at once. Colin had fought against the urge to comfort her. For reasons he couldn't explain, he had every intention of keeping Melissa with her daughter, together, where they belonged, and helping her put this entire mess with Richard behind her.

"Are we good?" Colin asked Deputy Garcia. Colin had been in plenty of volatile situations before but never with a kid. Part of him thought he should've put up a stronger argument for Dallas taking the youngster to the ranch, where she'd be tucked away and safe. Colin didn't have to be a father to understand Melissa's need to keep her daughter in her arms, to protect her above all else. Melissa had had that desperate, determined look in her eyes. The kind only a devoted mother could have. So, he'd figure out a way to take them both on the run and keep them safe. He needed to account for the baby being with them because that complicated the situation. Based on his knowledge from the kiddos at the ranch, the younger the baby, the more the feedings occurred. It would be more difficult to travel with one so little.

Garcia nodded. "I can't force anyone into protective custody. It's her choice. It's my job to advise against this course of action. Obviously, I won't stop you from leaving. I'm planning to get some air myself. I'm going to step outside via the...?" He looked at Colin.

"ER bay," he said. Colin understood the insinuation. Garcia was giving them an out while he watched over them to make sure they made it safely out of the parking lot.

"My truck will be waiting," Dallas said with a nod, emptying the cash from his pockets and handing over a stack of twenties. "This should help. There's a baby seat inside the truck that should work fine for the little one."

Colin was grateful for the help.

Garcia checked his watch. "If I head out now I'll be back in five minutes or so."

"Thank you," Colin said. Leaving Tommy while he was in the hospital fighting for his life was a tough blow. The image of his friend being shot and bleeding out in a parking lot would stick with Colin for a long time.

Being negative and fearing the worst wasn't the energy he wanted to put into the situation.

Thoughts were powerful. Colin replaced the image with the two of them fishing together this summer, smiling, drinking a cold brew. Tommy would pull through, *had* to pull through.

"Make sure he has everything he needs when he wakes from surgery." Colin nodded toward the hallway, thinking that he needed to stop off at a gas station so that he could pick up a pre-paid phone—one that couldn't be traced back to him—so that he could check on Tommy.

"Will do." Garcia tipped his hat before walking out of the room.

"You ready?" he asked Melissa.

She nodded. "Angelina's diaper bag is in my car. It has everything I need to get through a couple of days."

"I'll put it in the truck if you tell me where you're parked and give me the keys," Dallas said.

Melissa's hand trembled but she managed to locate her keys and hand them over. "I'm parked in the visitor lot. Front row. White car. I don't know the license plate and I can't remember if there's more than one."

"I can use the auto-lock button to locate it," he said. "Give me a head start, a couple of minutes."

Colin drained his coffee cup and then set it on the counter.

Melissa had given her baby a pacifier and that had settled her down. Melissa's nerves, on the other hand, were raw. She never paced and she was practically wearing a hole in the blue carpet.

"Let's do this." Colin took Melissa's free hand and led her toward the stairs. He ignored the frisson of heat, figuring it was residual attraction left over from more than a year ago. He chalked it up to unfinished business between the two of them. Spending a few days with her while the feds caught up with Richard would be just what Colin needed to gain closure. He had to admit that seeing Melissa with her and Richard's daughter was going a long way toward helping him realize that she'd moved on. Did he have questions about Angelina? Yeah. This wasn't the time or the place to ask.

He led her to the ER bay, where the king cab truck waited, engine purring, keys inside.

"Keep your head down and walk with purpose," he said from the sterile white hallway. "No matter what happens, don't look up. I'll stand behind you as you buckle your daughter into the car seat and I'll make sure no one's taking notice of what you're doing. Do the best you can to act casual."

Colin tucked his chin to his chest so that the

brim of his Stetson would cover his face. He stood behind Melissa, his hand on the small of her back, as she tucked her little bundle in the car seat.

Soon after, she opened the front passenger door and climbed inside the vehicle without drawing unwanted attention. Knowing that Deputy Garcia had eyes on them to prevent any problems or in case things went south to give them extra time was a comfort. Dallas was no doubt keeping watch, as well. That was even more reassuring.

Pulling out of the lot, Colin kept vigilant watch on anything that moved around them. At this time of night, there was very little activity on the roads and that would make it a little more challenging to get out of town unnoticed. He needed to get them onto the highway pretty darn quick where they could blend in with the other vehicles. There were more trucks in this part of Texas than sedans, so being in Dallas's truck would help.

"Where are we going?" Melissa asked, fighting back a yawn.

Colin ignored the reaction his body had to the sadness and defeat in her voice. No doubt, she was exhausted. It was the middle of the night and there was no telling how long it had been since she'd had a good night's sleep. Her lack of rest most likely had more to do with the man she'd lived with than the baby sleeping in the backseat.

"Where's Richard from?" he asked, his eyes focused on the road ahead. He was already making his way toward the highway.

"Oklahoma City, originally. Why?" she asked, sounding surprised at the question.

"His family still there?" he asked, not ready to answer just yet. He meandered onto the highway, grateful for the thick traffic. He'd kept vigilant watch in the rearview mirror to make sure no one had followed them.

A cursory glance at her and he saw that her head was leaned against the headrest and her gaze was fixed out the front windshield. Her fingers pinched her nose like she was trying to stem a headache.

"Yes," she said.

"Then, we're headed to Oklahoma City," he said.

"What? Why?" she asked as she turned to face him.

"Because it's the last place he'll expect you to be while we formulate a plan," he said.

"Shouldn't we be running anywhere besides his hometown?" she asked.

"He won't expect us to go there. And he needs to know we're not in Bluff anymore.

Word will get around." Colin checked the rearview again to see if any cars were following them. "I'll need to find a place that we can bunk down with a baby for a few days. We'll need more supplies than what's in your diaper bag."

Dallas had a gun permit so there'd be a gun in the locked glove compartment. He'd cleared out his shotgun from the backseat once he'd had a baby.

Colin always carried cash, and he had a couple hundred dollars in his wallet plus what Dallas had given him.

"We'll have to stay off the grid, which means no credit cards. I have enough money to get by until we figure out a plan of attack. First step is to get us to a secure area and far away from Bluff. A place that your husband will least suspect to find you."

"Should we figure out a way to let Richard see us leaving?" she asked.

"Too risky," he said.

Melissa got quiet like she did when she was churning something over and over again in her mind. Reasoning with her when she was doing that wouldn't do any good, so Colin focused on his own thoughts.

When he was sure they were in the clear, he stopped off at a gas station to buy a cell phone.

A little while later, Colin wasn't exactly sure when, Melissa settled into her chair. She leaned back and rubbed her temples. A short time after that, her breathing became steady and even.

The baby in the backseat stirred but didn't cry. He thought about her curly black hair and that face…

Colin pushed the image of the little girl out of his mind as he made the rest of the almost four-hour drive. He veered east to Lake Stanley Draper and then located a boat dock. After scouting for a good place to bunk for the night, he parked the vehicle just inside a few trees in order to keep the truck out of sight. The sun would be up soon and he'd watch the dock throughout the next morning to see who came and went. This time of year and with rain in the forecast, he hoped no one would show and they could have their pick of houseboat rentals to "borrow."

His brain hadn't had time to process the fact that Melissa was in his life again, even if it was temporary. He looked over at her and his heart fisted—not the reaction he was hoping for.

Since they were going to be around each other 24/7, at least for a few days, he needed a mental headshake to stay on track. Because seeing her asleep and looking so vulnerable was threatening to crack the walls he'd constructed around his heart.

She was resting peacefully and he didn't want to disturb her, so he took care in leaning her chair back and then pulled a blanket Dallas kept in the backseat and placed it over her. She rolled onto her side but didn't open her eyes.

His military training made it easy for him to sleep anywhere, anytime. Working the ranch had reinforced his need for very little shut-eye. A couple hours of quality time would be good enough for him. The sun would be up soon and that would make it harder to rest. He closed his eyes and the image of Melissa's little girl immediately popped into his thoughts.

Curly black hair. Those round cheeks. The name, Angelina.

Couldn't be his, he thought as he settled in so he could nab a few hours of shut-eye.

Chapter Six

All Colin would've needed was a couple hours of sleep and he'd be good to go. He got forty-five minutes before the little angel in the backseat stirred, waking him. He sat up and surveyed his surroundings. The wind was picking up. Other than slight movement in the trees, all seemed quiet.

And that's when his brain decided to loop the notion that Angelina looked a lot like him from his own baby pictures.

With effort, he pushed aside the image. Didn't need that distraction this morning. Besides, Richard had dark hair and Angelina was his daughter.

Melissa was still asleep but Colin needed coffee. There was no way he could wake her even though he suspected the little one would be up soon enough for a feeding.

Caffeine would go a long way toward clearing the cobwebs in his head. Colin shook his head to see if that would do any good. Maybe going over what he knew so far would get his blood pumping. Just the thought of Richard Rancic was enough to heat Colin's blood. There was enough residual anger there to do the trick, and the notion that the man had targeted Melissa stoked the flames.

Colin couldn't go there without questioning the circumstances under which Melissa had walked out on him in the first place. Had she known what she was getting into when she'd made that choice? Richard had been all flash and charm as he'd rolled through town, and Colin had been beyond shocked when Melissa had fallen for it, for him. He'd believed that the two of them were solid, that nothing could come between them, which seemed pretty naive now.

Apparently, money could. There was no way Melissa could have had real feelings for Richard, was there?

Sure, her father had been having some business troubles. That much was common knowledge. Had Rancic made promises to Mr. Roark, to Melissa after going into business with him? Mr. Roark loved his daughter and his lack of business acumen was well-known in some circles. Had he played a role in the sudden turn of events last year? Had money?

Those were questions that Colin wouldn't allow himself to consider. He'd made his decision to move on that rainy spring day when she'd thrown his ring at him. Afterward, he'd shut down all communication between them, which wasn't too difficult given that she'd moved and he'd never been on social media. Besides, he wasn't one to hang around where he wasn't wanted.

The way Richard had made his family's wealth so obvious had turned Colin's stomach. Sure, Colin had money, too. To him, his family fortune amounted to a bunch of zeroes in a bank account. Security was nice, don't get him wrong, but he didn't need much beyond the basics of oxygen, water, food, shelter and sleep. Three of those cost nothing, considering his water came from various wells on the ranch. Then, there was the obvious need for companionship, for building a life with someone.

Colin looked at Melissa, the woman who felt so much like a stranger. Change was inevitable. More than a year had passed since he'd last seen her. She was a mother now. And yet what he'd seen in her eyes last night was the result of something totally different. She'd been in what he could only guess was an abusive marriage. There were no physical marks that he could see but that didn't mean much. His charity work with victims had given him insight into what went on behind closed doors in toxic relationships. He'd listened to countless victims talk about how good they became at hiding bruises. And then there was emotional abuse, the kind that left no visible trail but did as much, if not more, damage on the inside. He found it painful to watch people stay in unhealthy relationships. He wanted them to know there was a way out, but he knew they'd see only when they were able to, if at all.

And what about the baby? A man who would strike down an officer of the law didn't seem like the type to let his child go. No matter what else happened, Richard would always be the girl's father. The little bundle in the backseat would bind Melissa to Richard for the rest of her life.

Even if she hadn't seen through Richard right away, how could Melissa be so careless as to have a baby with someone she barely knew? Then again, the same wisdom carried over to her choice to marry the man in the first place. Colin wouldn't understand it in a hundred years. Melissa had been clear with him. She'd thought they were too young to have a child when he'd thrown the idea out. She'd said that she wanted to have time together to build memories of the two of them before expanding their family. He'd argued that they'd been dating for two years already. He knew enough about her to realize that she was the one, the only one he wanted to spend the rest of his life with. He didn't need a marriage certificate to have a baby. Although, he knew that she did and respected it. A blow, like a physical punch, nearly knocked the wind out of him at thinking about her having a child with Richard.

Where'd that come from?

It's exactly what he deserved for rehashing the past, he thought wryly.

What's done was done. There was no going back and no changing it. Colin accepted that logically even if his heart had some catching up to do.

Melissa rolled onto her side and then opened her eyes. Still that same honey-brown with violet streaks.

"Morning," he said quietly, not wanting to wake the little passenger in the backseat.

Melissa stretched and yawned, immediately checking behind her. "Already time to wake up?"

"Afraid so," he said.

"Where are we?" She pulled the lever on

her chair in order to sit upright and then spun around to check on her daughter.

"East of Oklahoma City," he supplied, straightening out his own chair. Even the large cab in the vehicle had been uncomfortable for a man of his size and build. "I need coffee. Will it wake her if I drive to the store?"

"Car rides actually help her sleep," she said. "I can heat a bottle at the store when she wakes."

He rubbed his eyes as he started the ignition.

Melissa was quiet on the drive to the country market. The baby started shifting around and he figured it was only a matter of time before she started crying.

Fifteen minutes later, he pulled into a spot and parked.

"Should I wait here for you or can I take her into the bathroom to change her?" she asked, adding, "She'll need to eat soon, too."

"What do you need for that?" He'd been around enough babies in the past few months to know they ate different things at different times based on their ages.

"I have formula in her diaper bag, so maybe just clean water and a microwave to warm it up," she said, and then lowered her voice when she added, "I couldn't breastfeed."

The note of sadness in her voice at that last

part struck him in a bad place. The main task of a mother, in his opinion, was to love her child unconditionally. Colin could see that wasn't a problem for Melissa. She might not have been ready to be a mother, but from what he'd seen so far she'd more than stepped up to the challenge. He'd seen the way she looked at her baby last night. The fierce protectiveness in her eyes. An irritating little voice in the back of his head said that she might not have been ready to be a parent *with him*.

Colin glanced around. "Since we're fairly close to his family home, you should stick near me while we're exposed."

He waited while she unbuckled the baby and the little girl's sleepy yawn tugged at his heart.

Inside, he bought a couple of travel toothbrushes and a tube of toothpaste and then waited for Melissa in the hallway leading to the restroom while she changed her daughter. He could hear her low voice as she sang to the infant.

A couple of minutes later, she opened the door. The baby was swaddled in a pink blanket and all he could see clearly was her sweet little face and those round eyes.

"I bought a few supplies I thought you might appreciate considering how fast we left town," he said, holding up the offerings, remembering how quickly she would hop out of bed to brush her teeth in the mornings. Then again, most of the time she hopped right back in afterward for a heated round of making love before she had to get ready for work.

"Can you hold her while I brush?" Her smile faded fast as she looked at him and then at the baby. There was a mix of emotions he couldn't readily identify brewing behind her eyes.

"Sure." He held out his arms. He'd had enough experience holding babies at the ranch in the past six months to make him feel comfortable enough with Angelina. Instead of focusing on the fact that this was Richard's daughter, he thought about her belonging to Melissa and a feeling of the world being right came over him as he took her. It was odd.

He'd always known that Melissa would be a good mother, even when she didn't have the confidence to believe in herself. From what he could see so far, Angelina was happy, content. Melissa had done well.

"Will you be okay?" she asked. Her desperate and panicked look was almost an insult.

It shouldn't make him smile, but it did. He also shouldn't feel a surge of attraction toward Melissa but he felt that, too. His heart warned that spending time with her was going to take a toll.

"I'm fine. Not sure how she feels about all this—" he glanced down at the baby and back "—but I'm good."

Melissa's eyes gave away her nervousness. She didn't leave. Instead, she shifted her weight from foot to foot and he could tell that she was analyzing her options. "Maybe I should just figure out a way—"

"I got this. Go brush," he said, nodding toward the restroom.

She chewed on the thought for a minute, glancing from him to her daughter.

"I'll be back in one sec," she finally said, holding up her index finger.

"Go," he repeated.

She blew out a breath and immediately disappeared into the bathroom.

The door flew open a few minutes later and she came out with her hair in a ponytail and a fresh face. "I'll take her back now."

She seemed especially nervous for him to be holding her daughter. He cocked an eyebrow but didn't call her out on it, chalking it up to being too close to Rancic's family home as he handed Angelina over to her mother.

Colin excused himself to go to the men's room and brush his teeth, and then bought two cups of steaming brew. Melissa liked sweeteners added to hers but Colin liked his straight-up black.

She smiled when she saw the cup meant for her. "That looks amazing right now. But she gets hers first."

"What can I do to help?" he asked.

She gave him a couple of instructions, so he went inside to use the microwave. When he mixed the warm water with the formula and it looked like milk, he let himself smile.

"You're actually pretty good at that," she said, bouncing her baby, who was sucking away on a pacifier.

There was a moment happening between them, a connection that he couldn't afford. He handed over the bottle. "Wait here until I come get you."

"Okay." She started the feeding.

Colin walked away, climbed into the cab and started the truck. He didn't move far. He repositioned the truck at one side of the parking lot where he could watch all the vehicles exiting the highway. It made him visible, too, so he slipped on his cowboy hat and shades even though the skies were starting to cloud up. He'd rather have Melissa and the baby as much out of sight as possible.

As he walked toward the convenience mart, Melissa met him halfway.

"Can you sit in the backseat and feed her?" he asked.

"Yes," she said. Once the baby was settled in with the bottle, Melissa said, "Colin."

There was something in her voice he couldn't quite pinpoint, maybe a warning, that had him thinking her next words weren't going to be ones that he wanted to hear.

"Yeah," was all he said, resisting the urge to look at her through the rearview mirror. His head already pounded and he didn't need to add to that.

"Thank you for everything you're doing for me and Angelina. I'm really sorry about what happened between us before," Melissa finally said.

There was a long pause. Another reason not to get too comfortable in their tentative…alliance. Friendship was too strong a word. He was helping someone who needed him. That's as far as Colin would allow his mind to go with this.

"It is what it is," he countered, not able to go there with her. Call it licking wounds or whatever, but he had no plans to use this time to "reconnect" their relationship. Richard had won. She'd married him instead of Colin. There was nothing more that needed to be said between them. "Let's just stay focused on what needs to be done and get you two moved on."

"Okay," she said, a little breathless.

Had he knocked the wind out of her with his cold shoulder? Maybe. It was nothing compared to the blow she'd delivered him a year ago.

"Where to next?" she asked after the baby finished her bottle and had been burped.

"We need to find a place to bunk down for the night and get out of the open," he said. "Then, I'll make sure we have enough supplies to get us through tonight since I plan on staying put."

He pulled out the cell he'd bought.

"Where'd you get that?" she asked.

"At a convenience store last night. It's a throw-away phone, meaning there's no way to trace it back to us. I paid cash for it so the transaction can't be tracked back to us, either," he supplied. Sticking to the facts and keeping conversation to a minimum should help keep her from confusing his help for still having feelings for her.

"I must've slept right through all of that," she said.

"I had to stop for gas and I wanted to call the hospital to check on Tommy," he said.

"And?"

"He made it out of surgery not long after we left last night. Everything went well and the doctor was able to remove all the bullet fragments from the shotgun blast," he replied.

"That's so good to hear," she said on an expelled breath. "I'm so relieved."

"He lost a lot of blood but, yeah, he'll pull through. He's tough," Colin said.

Tears streamed down her cheeks and Colin resisted the urge to reach over and wipe them away. It was muscle memory and nothing more causing him to want to do that.

"Richard doesn't want anything to do with Tommy. He just happened to get in the way, so he should be safe from any retaliation," she said.

"There will be enough eyes on Tommy's room to make sure of it. Plus, your husband killed a law enforcement officer. No one takes that lightly," he said with a little more intensity than he'd planned.

"It's good we left town. I don't want anyone else getting hurt because of me," she said. Was she blaming herself?

"It's because of Richard, not you. *You* had nothing to do with this." Colin gripped the steering wheel tighter.

"Yes, I did. I knew better than to come back to Bluff. Marshal Davis is dead because

I didn't listen to him. He warned me against returning. I heard Richard was last seen heading to Canada, so I went against his advice. There's no way that his death is not my fault," she said, and Colin tried not to notice how much anguish there was in her voice. Shock still reverberated through him at just how dangerous the man she'd married seemed to be.

"Tell me about your husband, Melissa. What's he into?" he asked.

"I don't even know where to start. He's a career criminal."

"And you had no idea before you rushed into marriage with him?" Colin's voice was too harsh and she immediately went into defensive mode.

"Remember when I took you on that fishing trip to Big Bend?" he asked.

Her cheeks flushed and he realized just what part of the trip she'd focused on. Yes, they'd had hours and hours of great sex, but that wasn't where he was going with this.

"The sun was going down. You were sitting out on the porch and there was that baby jackrabbit that you thought lost its mother. You put tiny pieces of vegetables along one end of the porch. The jackrabbit came over and you thought it was the cutest little thing. You were so happy that you'd fed it and then so startled when an eagle swooped down and snapped up the jackrabbit. You made yourself sick over blaming yourself for that little creature's death."

"That was obviously my fault, Colin. If I hadn't fed the jackrabbit it would be alive today."

"There's where you're wrong. That eagle would've been flying around anyway. He would've seen the jackrabbit and swooped down to get him no matter what. That's his nature and you're not responsible for that," Colin said, hoping his words might offer some reassurance.

She gave a noncommittal shrug in response.

EVERYWHERE MELISSA HAD GONE, everything she'd done for the past year made her feel like she was the jackrabbit and her husband was the eagle. There was always the thought of him lurking in the back of her mind, ready to swoop down and take Angelina away. Even when he left on business—and those were trips that had kept her sane—there was never a feeling that he was ever truly gone.

The fear that he'd pop up around every corner had almost driven her beyond the brink. Once the baby had been born, Melissa had kept Angelina within arm's reach at all times.

Always aware that Richard could put two and two together at any moment and deliver on his threats to destroy Melissa and everyone she loved if she betrayed him.

And now she really was the jackrabbit, seeking shelter, scrambling to get away from the eagle that was circling, ready to pounce the second she slipped. Any mistake and she'd be in the eagle's grip, where she'd be crushed.

Colin pulled into the spot near the trees where they'd been parked this morning. She sipped on her coffee, wishing it could give her more than a fleeting jolt of energy.

"What is he wanted for?" Colin asked.

"The feds are after him for money laundering and murder. Also, he was using his resorts as a shelter in order to harbor some very bad men, keeping them hidden from law enforcement and allowing them access to the US. His brother is involved in the business and I think his father is, too, but I couldn't find proof," she said.

"How do you know about his brother?" he asked.

"I recorded them during their Sunday night football games. They used to turn up the volume real loud so feds sitting out front in a white minivan couldn't pick up their voices when the two of them talked business. I sewed a recording device inside the collar of one of Richard's shirts. He always wore a button-down. Even on game day," she said.

"How'd you know which shirt he would wear?" he asked.

"I didn't. So, I sewed it into the collar of one of his favorites and waited." She didn't want to think about all those sleepless nights she'd spent waiting for him to wear the right shirt. There were too many.

"That was taking a big risk," Colin said with a hint of reverence in his voice. She didn't want to notice. She didn't want to think about how much she'd missed his deep voice—a voice that could soothe even the worst days. His easygoing style could lift her up the minute she saw him. He'd been her safe place. Her shelter from all the craziness of trying to stay on top of her father's affairs. Obviously, she'd failed at that, too, or she wouldn't be in this mess in the first place.

"I should've done more," she said, thinking of the mix of excitement and tension she'd had the Sunday morning she'd finally seen Richard wearing the shirt. The sense of freedom that was so close she could almost touch it. It had been like standing in the middle of a downpour with a bolt of sunlight on the horizon.

No matter what, she'd had to control her reaction. Even though she'd had a lot of training at stuffing her feelings down deep inside, nothing had prepared her for the mix of nerves on that day. She'd been so relieved that the nightmare was nearing an end and yet so anxious that something would go wrong and he'd figure her out before the feds could get what they needed to arrest him.

Knowing just how much was at stake made the task even more difficult.

"You played it right. You did the right things," he said. "I know it probably doesn't feel like it right now. But you did."

"Did I?" she asked, fierce and angry at the same time. "I was afraid, so federal officers had to put a lot of pressure on me to get a recording, or some kind of admission from him about his illegal activities. Talking to him about what he did when he left the house wasn't even a serious consideration for me. He would've known something was up immediately and I didn't dare risk Angelina's life. But my daughter's life is in danger because I failed her."

"Don't think like that, Melissa." His words brought little comfort when she thought about everything that could go wrong. "We'll figure this out. Her father will be in jail for the rest of his life. He won't be able to hurt her."

Hearing Colin say those words knifed her.

She wanted to scream that Richard wasn't the father. This wasn't the right time to have the discussion that she needed to have with Colin about her daughter's paternity. She needed to change the subject. "How do we find shelter?"

"By being patient," he said.

"I don't know how much longer I can sit here and do nothing while my life crumbles around me. I've done too much of that already," she said, and then figured she'd said too much based on Colin's reaction. She made a move for the door handle.

"Where do you think you're going?" he asked.

"I can't sit here anymore," she said.

"You need to take a walk? Get some fresh air?" he asked, his voice rising in anger. "Then get used to someone being right on top of you because you're not getting out of my sight until this situation is resolved. You've run out of patience? Good. So have I, and I won't tolerate anyone stalking out on their own and disappearing on me, especially not since you've done it once already."

Chapter Seven

Melissa froze. Her heart thudded. Her chest squeezed. All Colin needed to add in order to complete the insult would be to remind her that it was her own fault she was in this mess. He could tell her that she should've handled everything differently. She should've trusted him and talked to him about it earlier. She should've...

Going down that road again was as productive as milking a bat to feed a horse. Another round of the blame game wouldn't change anything. All she'd be doing was wasting precious energy, and she needed every ounce to get her through this ordeal.

Out of her peripheral vision, she could see Colin chewing on his jaw like he did when he said something he regretted. He'd always acted on impulse and could rely on his charm to get him out of sticky situations. That was part of the reason she hadn't confided in him before. She couldn't be sure that he wouldn't do something they'd all regret.

He had no idea what she'd faced. And he had no idea the real reasons she'd married Richard. She almost blurted out that she'd made those choices in order to protect him and his family. What good would it do? Colin would never forgive her for walking out. He'd never get over what she'd done, especially not when he learned that Angelina was his daughter. So, there was no use in trying to pretend otherwise. Let him believe what he believed. The truth would only hurt him more.

Besides, she'd had her father to protect. He was finally in protective custody, being cared for in a nursing home. Once this was over, she and Angelina could settle into a little house. Bring her father there. She could get a job.

Part of her almost wished she'd skimmed money from the piles of cash Richard always had on hand. If she'd needed proof that Richard had been involved in illegal activity, it hadn't taken long to figure out. Who put tens of thousands of dollars out on the breakfast table?

She'd suspected foul play after the first couple of weeks of marriage, and it hadn't taken long to realize that he was knee-deep in illegal activity. Of course, there'd been no preparing her for just how demented her husband was or how far he was willing to go to keep his activities quiet.

"We'll camp out here for the rest of the day and keep an eye on the dock," Colin finally said, cutting into her heavy thoughts. He pointed to a spot between the trees.

Melissa focused. At first she didn't see anything but then it became clear. She saw several large boats. She had never spent much time in the water and she had a lifelong fear of drowning, so she had no idea what kind of boats she was looking at except to say that they offered shelter. A few were large. Houseboats?

"I can't sleep on one of those," she said. "You know I'm terrified of drowning."

"Did your husband know that, too?" Colin asked.

"Yes." Hearing Colin say the words *your husband* sat heavy in her chest. In her mind, Richard had never been her husband.

"Then it's the safest place for us to be. He'd never look for you around water," he said, and he was right. It was smart and she hoped she could actually do it.

"That might be true but—"

"I won't let anything happen to you, but you have to trust me."

That was a tall order. She trusted Colin

without a doubt. It was the water she didn't trust. Her pulse kicked up just thinking about it. How many times had she been startled out of a deep sleep with the nightmare that she was drowning? Too many. But if facing her fear meant protecting her daughter, there was nothing to think about.

"You're right about all of it," she conceded, glancing up at the skies that had darkened under layers of gray clouds. "How long do we wait?"

"Until nightfall. I have my eye on that one." He pointed toward a cream-colored boat with a blue zigzag stripe down the side. "My guess is that it's a rental, which means we'll have to clear out around nine o'clock every morning just to be safe. We should be okay this time of year since there are no major school breaks. There'll be fewer vacationers to worry about."

"How do you know that?"

"It's the same on the ranch for the Rifleman's Club. We see the most visitors during school breaks in March. Other than that, we get a few stragglers, mostly honeymooners and guys' trips."

"I never understood honeymooners going on a hunting vacation," she said. "To each his own, I guess."

"Women in Texas know how to handle a

rifle," he said, and there was a disapproving quality to his tone. "And they like to shoot."

"I know and I get it. But on your honeymoon? I can think of better things to do than shoot wild hogs," she said.

Out of the corner of her eye, she saw Colin's muscles tense. It dawned on her that he must be thinking about her own honeymoon. The one she never had and didn't want in the first place. "It's not like that. I…"

"Save it," he said under his breath. There was so much anger behind those two words.

How many nights in the past year had she stayed awake, wondering how much he hated her for what she'd done? The mystery was over. It was clear and so hard to see because she never stopped loving him, not even now. Her heart didn't care or seem to want to acknowledge there was no going back. Not with Colin. She'd known that when she walked away and yet seeing it written all over his expression and hearing it in his words made it seem so…final.

She'd done what she had to do in order to survive, she reminded herself. Repeating her mantra had gotten her through so many difficult times in her life.

Naively, she'd believed that given enough time she'd get over Colin. How young. How silly. Maybe there was one true love in life and if it didn't work out, that was it. She tried not to let the thought deflate her. Besides, Angelina was her heart now. Melissa had her daughter and a piece of Colin would be with her forever. That had been enough to get her through an entire year with Richard. It would be enough to carry her through the rest of her life, as well.

Angelina was already showing signs of her father's personality. Smart. Stubborn. Independent. Sometimes a little intense. And her face? She had the face of an angel.

Melissa needed to change the subject.

"I hate not knowing what's going on in Bluff," Melissa said.

Colin took a minute to answer. "We'll find out when we call the hospital to check on Tommy in a little while."

"Can we do that?" she asked.

"Calls go through a switchboard, so the numbers are impossible to trace. One of my brothers will be in the room and should pick up."

"Tommy's safe, right? In case Richard changes his mind and goes after him for answers," she asked, giving into a moment of panic. "Richard can't get to him, can he?"

"Not with my brothers on watch and as we already covered Richard was never after Tommy. Besides, with him being spotted in the area someone will keep eye on Tommy at all times. I doubt Richard would be crazy enough to try anything else in Bluff. It'd be too risky and he's fixated on getting to you. He'd only make a move on Tommy's room if he thought you were there," Colin said. "I'm sure he's figured out by now that you're nowhere around town."

"How? He didn't see me leave," she said, and the thought of seeing Richard again caused her pulse to race.

"You haven't been spotted, either. You've had a run-in with him, so he's cunning enough to realize that you'd bolt. He's figuring that you're scared, so he's most likely having someone watch the ranch just in case you come running back to me."

"He knows that I wouldn't do that," she said in a moment of fear. The words came out a little too quickly based on Colin's reaction. She needed to make something up or he'd start asking questions, and she didn't have the heart to hurt him again with what she knew about his father. News like that would devastate the O'Briens and they'd always been good to her. There was no way she would deliver that blow to the proud family. "Richard was convinced that I was still in love with you when we married. So, I had to go to great lengths to prove to him that I'd gotten over you."

"And he believed you?" he said, staring out the front windshield, his arms folded across his chest.

"Of course he did. It took some time but I finally convinced him. I made sure there was no room for doubt." She left out the part where both her and her daughter's survival had depended on her putting on a convincing show.

"How soon did you figure out he's a criminal?" Colin asked. He'd recovered his game face and his voice gave away nothing of his emotions. This was a new side to him, a side that she couldn't read. Maybe it had been there all along but she'd never seen it. Before, she believed that the two of them had shared everything. With him, she could truly be herself. No pretense. No facade. Just Melissa. Imperfections and all. And he'd seemed to love her even more for them. But then he'd always been black-and-white. If Colin loved something, he went all in.

Pain gripped her. She had to breathe through it and not allow the walls to collapse around her like it had felt so many times in the past year. It was so much harder to construct barriers with Colin sitting right next to her.

"It didn't take long." She'd known since before the wedding that something was off with Richard, but it didn't matter because her priority had been to protect her father and Colin.

"And you stayed anyway?" he asked. The note of disappointment in his tone was a knife to her heart.

If she was going to get through this with him, and there was no other choice at the moment, then she was going to have to turn off her feelings altogether. She straightened in her chair and stared out the window. She hated the thought of lying. Period. And lying to Colin was even worse.

"I had a daughter to think about." That wasn't a lie.

"How soon did you get pregnant after leaving me?" he asked, and he didn't seem able to hide the bitterness.

"I'm hungry." She didn't dare look at him because he'd see the tears welling in her eyes. There was no way she could afford to give away her emotions now. "When's lunch?"

"We're not leaving until you tell me the truth. You said that you weren't ready to have a baby with me. And yet you seemed perfectly fine to have a child with a man that you knew was a criminal? None of this makes sense to me, Melissa."

"Can't we just leave it at that?" she asked. Her carefully constructed walls were cracking.

"No." The power of that one word struck her.

Colin had questions. She knew that. She'd seen it in his eyes from the moment he got a good look at her daughter.

"Well, I'm not talking about it," she said with as much authority as she could muster.

"Why not?" he asked.

"Because…"

"You hate me that much?" There was so much anger and pain in his voice.

"It's not that…"

"Then what, Melissa?" His gaze bore holes into her.

"Leave it alone." He would do the math at some point and realize…oh, no. He would figure out that Angelina was his daughter. And then what? Would he want to keep her and push Melissa away? He'd never forgive her. She'd seen the hurt and anger buried deep in his eyes and there'd be no coming back from that. Even so, a little voice in her head said that he deserved to know. That Angelina deserved to know her real father.

"What if I can't?" he said quietly and with so much hurt in his voice. "What if I need to know so I can move on? I need to hear it, Melissa. I need to hear that you loved him when you walked out. That you didn't leave me for some…rich jerk…with a bent for breaking the law."

"That's why you thought I left?" His words were daggers to her chest.

"What am I supposed to think?" he asked.

"I didn't have a choice. I was forced to leave. Does knowing that really make you feel better?" she blurted out, and then folded her arms across her chest.

"Maybe." His gaze flicked from Angelina back to Melissa and she could tell that he was about to ask the question she feared most…

"Is she mine?"

Melissa looked down at her angel. She needed to stay strong for Angelina, so she took a fortifying breath. This wasn't the way she'd imagined telling Colin that he was a father, but she didn't have it in her heart to lie to him anymore, either.

"Yes." She couldn't look at him.

All she heard was a sharp intake of air before the driver's side door opened and then closed.

In that moment she knew that everything had changed.

Melissa waited a full twenty minutes before she slipped out of the car. She cradled Angelina, who was happily cooing. She looked down at her baby, all big eyes and smiles. No matter the backlash she would face, it felt right to tell Colin. He deserved to know this angel belonged to him.

She found him sitting by the lake near the tree line, where he almost disappeared into the brush. He was staring out at the water, wearing an intense expression.

She almost didn't walk over to him.

But it was Colin. She'd just dropped a bomb on him and she deserved whatever backlash came with it.

"Can I sit with you?" she asked, stepping up beside him.

He didn't look up. His nod was almost imperceptible. She took it as a positive sign and sat down with enough distance between them to give him space.

If Angelina picked up on the tension between them she sure didn't act like it. She smiled and cooed at Melissa.

"I'm sorry that you're finding out like this," she said. "I'd planned—"

"What? To send me a postcard? From where? Was I ever going to get to know that I have a child?" It was obvious that Colin was keeping control of his temper because of the baby by the way his voice would start rising and then he'd glance at Angelina before pulling his emotions back into check. "I can read

the writing on the wall, Melissa. The reason
you were meeting with Marshal Davis was to
go into witness protection to get away from
Richard. I also know that you would never be
able to leave the program. Not as long as he or
his brother was alive. They'd hunt you down
and—" he glanced at the baby "—let's just say
there'd be no going back once you entered the
program. And did you think about her growing up without a father? How could you do that
to her? To me?"

This wasn't the time to tell him how often
she'd wake from a dream crying because of
how much she missed him. Or how many
times her heart begged to see him in the past
year. How much it had broken her spirit to
walk away in the first place and then to be
made to live with the charade that she actually
had feelings for another man. She had feelings
all right. As far as Richard went, none of them
were good.

There was no way she could make hearing
this news in this way right for Colin. When
other words escaped her, she finally asked,
"Do you want to hold your daughter?"

He shook his head.

Colin had stopped talking and that wasn't
a good sign.

The truth was out and Melissa couldn't bring

herself to regret it now. There was no changing it, no going back, no do-overs when it came to life. She'd done the best she could under the circumstances. Her decision had spared her father jail time in his last years. He was resting comfortably in an undisclosed facility. It had spared Colin's family shame and embarrassment. And their daughter was safe *for now*.

Chapter Eight

Storm clouds thickened as the day went on. The winds had picked up speed. It was obvious that a storm was brewing. Melissa wondered just how bad it was going to get. Thoughts of being on a boat during a bad storm weren't exactly warm and fuzzy.

Few words passed between Colin and Melissa for the balance of the day. He needed time to think, to process, and she understood that on some level. A bomb had been dropped and he was trying to get his bearings. She'd felt the same way. At first, she'd been shocked. And then, afraid.

When it came to Colin, there were worse things he could do besides give her the silent treatment. All things considered, this was good.

"The cream-colored boat with the blue stripe

will work for us," he finally said, motioning toward one of the vessels.

The thought of staying on a boat shot Melissa's heart rate up. She had second thoughts as panic gripped her.

"I can't do it. I can't get on that thing," she said, cradling Angelina close to her chest. "There has to be somewhere else we can go."

"This is the best place for all three of us," Colin said evenly, his tone unreadable.

She looked up at the cloudy sky. "It's going to rain."

"Uh-huh," he said, his gaze steady on her.

"You know how I feel about being anywhere near water, let alone on a lake during a storm," she said.

"It could get pretty bad tonight," he agreed.

"Come on, Colin. You don't expect me to…"

"What? Inconvenience yourself?" He fired the words like bullets from a silencer, quiet but deadly.

Tears threatened. "You know it's more than that."

She'd been deathly afraid of water since she was ten and stood ankle deep on the beach as her mother was swept away by a current while swimming during their annual trip to Gulf Shores, Alabama. Her mother's body had been found two days later. Since then, Melissa didn't go near the water.

"You need to decide what you're going to do, but me and that little girl will be on the boat tonight," he said, pushing up to stand.

Melissa stood and backed away from the water.

"You coming?" Colin held his hand out.

"It's not ours," she said. "What if we get caught?"

"We're just borrowing it. I'll have it back and in better condition than before when this is all said and done," he said, still standing, hand still extended.

He was a man of his word, and Melissa had no doubt that the owners would end up with something even nicer for their inconvenience. She was stalling, praying for courage.

"It's the only place she'll be safe tonight," he said, and his voice was low, compassionate as he motioned toward Angelina.

Melissa stared at her daughter's sweet round face. She looked out at the water and took a deep breath. "Okay."

She followed Colin to the dock.

"This is a rental and I already checked that they have everything we'll need to take care of her," he said as he held out his hand.

She took a tentative step toward him and the

ground swayed under her feet. "I don't know if I can."

"Don't think about it," he said, his voice calmer and more reassuring this time. "Take my hand and then take two steps forward."

The wood decking in the slip felt solid. The boat did not. Besides, the winds were picking up. Who knew how bad the storm might get.

"I can't. Not while I'm holding the baby," she said.

Colin repositioned until he had one foot on the boat and the other on the decking.

"You won't fall. Not on my watch," he said, and his voice was low. There was so much promise in his words that she took a tentative step forward, keeping one foot on land. The boat shifted and her stomach felt like she'd just dropped down the first hill on a roller coaster. She lifted her foot, anchoring herself with her back foot. Her foot hovered above the boat's decking.

No more being afraid.

With a deep breath and Colin's strong hand on her back, guiding her, Melissa made the short hop onto the boat. She hugged Angelina even closer as she navigated the shaky ground.

"There's a place to sit, cook and eat on board," he said, guiding her toward the open glass doors at the back. "There's also a shower and a bedroom for you and the baby. They have a bassinet for guests to use, so I can set that up."

"There really is everything here," she said, glancing around the space. The houseboat had a simple layout and felt a little bit like a wide RV.

"And those?" She pointed to stairs.

"Don't worry about them. The top deck is open and has extra space for people who rent this to catch plenty of sunrays. We won't be using it," he said. "The kitchen is stocked with pans, plates and glasses. We can easily get by for a few nights on here."

"Will we stay right here?" She glanced back at the sliders, which was not a good idea because it made her head spin.

"Steady," Colin said, his strong hands on her, helping her to the counter where she could lean. Much of his earlier shock and anger had dissipated. He had that focus in his eyes, that intensity, if not the spark. "We'll find a good spot and drop anchor for the night."

Her stomach flipped in part because of his eyes on her. "What about filling up the tank?"

"Most owners have a policy that these have to be returned full, so that's no worry. Everything should be ready to go," he said.

"Are you familiar with this lake?" she asked.

"No. There'll be maps on board. I'll find a good place for us to spend the night," he said.

"Do we have to leave the dock?" Another wave of panic rushed through her. At least she was close to shore as long as they were parked in the slip.

"Yes. Once I get you and the baby settled I'll run out for supplies—"

She was shaking her head as she held on to the counter for dear life. Thankfully, Angelina was napping in her arms.

"Sit down." He guided her to the couch. "We'll need food for us and more formula for her," he said.

"You can't leave us alone on this…*thing.*" Her throat was dry.

"Just for an hour or so while I get—"

"No. We're coming with you," she said. "After the baby wakes and has her bottle we can all go." She stopped herself from saying as a family. She wasn't even sure where the thought came from. They were Angelina's parents but they were far from a family. It was most likely just a blast from the past, a hope for what might've been. It was her nerves and the stress of the situation causing her brain to go there and not her heart's desire.

He must've picked up on how rapidly her

pulse was rising when he said, "It'll be okay. We'll figure this out together."

"Promise me you won't disappear if I go into the bathroom or something," she said. She was being irrational but she couldn't help herself.

"I give you my word," he said with a look that said he absolutely meant it. There was something about that one look, those words that calmed her more than she knew better than to allow.

She nodded.

Colin checked drawers until he located a map of the lake and another of the surrounding area. He spread both out on the counter and then studied them with the intensity of a climber looking for a water source.

"She's quiet and she sleeps a lot. Is everything okay?" he asked, and she picked up on the note of uncertainty in his voice. Parenting was new to him.

"She's a good baby," Melissa said, thinking she was three months ahead on the learning curve.

"Does Richard know that she's mine?" he asked.

"No," she said a little too quickly. "It was in our best interest for me to convince him that she was his."

Colin's gaze intensified on the map splayed out in front of him.

"You mean in *your* best interest," he said.

THE TRIP FOR supplies was uneventful. Dinner was quiet and the mood was heavy. Colin had set up the bassinet in one corner of the living room so they could keep watch over the baby while she slept. Melissa had washed the baby, fed her and then put the sleeping girl in her temporary bed. She turned around and faced Colin, who was doing a final review of the maps, no doubt ready to push off land soon.

"We need to talk," she said, motioning toward the chairs in the dining area near the sliding doors at the back of the boat.

Colin turned around and folded his arms.

"Teach me how to fight," she said.

"We don't exactly have a lot of time to train," he said, and his tense posture made her believe he was expecting a different conversation.

"We can use whatever time we have together," she said, determined.

"Our time will be better spent coming up with a strategy to deal with your husband," he said.

Hearing the word *husband* come out of Colin's mouth hit Melissa harder than a physical punch and yet she had married Richard.

Technically, legally, she was still married to Richard even though her heart had never agreed.

But Richard didn't get to make her feel afraid anymore.

"I've had a lot of time to think about... *things*. I'm tired of feeling weak and like I can't defend myself. Surely, that makes sense to someone like you," she said, refusing to beg. If he didn't want to train her she'd figure out another way to learn. It was as simple as that.

"What do you think I'm here for?" he asked, a little indignant. "I'll handle whatever comes our way."

"I need to take care of myself." She stood and then stalked toward the door. "I thought you of all people would understand that."

Melissa stepped outside into the cool evening air and onto the decking. Seeing all that water around her made her nauseous and dizzy. She hopped onto stable ground and grabbed onto a beam that supported the overhead structure.

Emotions were a tidal wave building inside her. Thoughts of hiding, of playing along with Richard's plans for the past year ate away at her insides. Having to pretend everything was great when she was dying inside fueled the force of the crash that was to come. The waves were cresting and she needed an outlet.

Melissa glanced around before running onto the nearby bank. She crouched down and hugged her knees, looking across the water near the light from the boat dock. As her gaze traveled onto the waves she couldn't help but notice that there was so much darkness, so much unknown.

Richard had always liked to keep her guessing. He'd tell her that he was going on a business trip and would be away for a few days only to show up an hour later just to catch her off guard. There was always some excuse as to why the change in plans. Meeting canceled. Flight canceled. She knew the real reason was to check up on her and keep her on her toes. If she never knew when to expect him then she always had the feeling he could walk through the door at any minute. Too many months of her life had been spent in fear of that, of him.

Fury had her eyes burning with tears that needed release. It had been so very long since she'd allowed herself to really cry, to release all the pent-up emotions pressing against the dam she'd built inside. Twelve long months of trying to convince Richard that she loved him when her heart wanted to burst from the pain of leaving Colin. She'd had to hide the fact that she was mourning the loss of the only man she ever loved. Ever would love? She'd had to bury everything. Had that made her seem cold to the outside world? Probably. There was no denying the ice inside her chest—the ice wall that only Angelina had managed to crack, until seeing Colin again.

She thought about all the other times that Richard had said he was leaving for two days and then didn't return for a week or more. Those times were even worse. The persistent feeling that he could show at any second unannounced ensured that she wouldn't rest. She didn't dare pack or try to disappear because he could literally show up in a blink. A year. Twelve months. Every day had felt like a prison sentence, like being locked in solitary confinement. Protecting her father had been her initial marching order. And then Colin's father complicated the situation. Angelina had come along, giving Melissa a reason to live but also a reason to stay. As long as Richard had thought the baby was his, she was given everything she could want. The best doctor in Tyler. The best care. And the best part was that he'd left her alone physically. But if he'd suspected for one minute that Angelina wasn't his...

Melissa couldn't even go there. She gave into the sobs racking her shoulders in sweet release. She would give herself a minute to mourn all that could've been and the horrible mess that her life had become. And then she would pick up the shattered pieces of her soul and move on.

Wiping tears from her cheeks, she rolled onto her stomach and started doing push-ups. Exercising had been her one haven and Richard had commented that he liked her body to be strong, so he didn't stop her.

If she had to figure out how to fight him on her own, so be it.

One. Two. She pushed off the cold hard earth. Three. Four. She continued, counting as she pushed up and then released down.

She went on like that…counting, pushing, counting, pushing until her arms burned and she could scarcely lift herself off the ground anymore. Melissa rolled onto her back, exhausted, and tried to catch her breath. Her chest rose and fell rapidly and her heart pounded in her chest. This was the first time she'd felt alive since leaving Bluff a year ago.

Movement out of the corner of her eye caught her off guard. She repositioned onto her belly again in order to get a better look, keeping her head low to the ground.

The figure moved toward her from the opposite direction of the boat.

She pushed to her feet. "Stop."

A male stepped into the clearing and she saw that it was Colin.

"Dammit, Colin. Why did you sneak up on me?"

"I didn't. You were emotional, angry and didn't pay enough attention to your surroundings," he said.

"How do you know what I felt?" she asked defensively.

He shot her a look that said he knew her better than that.

Melissa sat down on the cold earth and cradled her legs against her chest, watching the houseboat. "And?"

"That made you vulnerable. You think fighting is about hitting someone, but a bullet beats a fist every time," he said as he sat next to her. He motioned toward the boat. "Angelina is asleep. If she wakes, we'll be able to hear her from here."

Heat radiated off him and her body flushed with him this close. His scent washed over her, virile and musky and clean. His knee touched hers and an explosion of electricity sparked between them. He must've felt it, too, because he repositioned so that they didn't make contact.

"Tell me everything about your husband," he

said. "The more I know, the better I can figure out how he'll come at us."

"First of all, I need you to stop calling him my husband," she said emphatically. "I was planning to divorce him."

It wasn't exactly the truth but she wouldn't have hesitated if the opportunity had arisen, and she'd been looking for an out from before she'd said *I do.*

"Why didn't you go to the police when you found out about his illegal activities?" Colin asked.

"I was afraid. He'd made it clear from day one of my pregnancy that if I ever went against him that losing my daughter would be the least of my worries," she said, keeping her gaze trained on the houseboat.

"So, he's the kind of guy who figures out what's important and then uses it against people. It also tells me that he isn't afraid to use his own flesh and blood to his advantage," he said. "Even though he thinks that Angelina is his, he would still use her against you."

If only Colin knew the extent to which Richard would make someone pay. Melissa nodded. "He has no soul."

"Then why get together with him in the first place?" he asked.

"My father. Richard threatened to have him jailed unless I married him."

"And you didn't think to come to me and talk about it?"

"There was nothing you could've done," she defended.

"We'll never know now." Colin paused. The flash of anger across his already intense features said that he was contemplating her words a little deeper. "Richard's desperate now. Anyone willing to shoot law enforcement doesn't feel like they have anything to lose. That will make him even more dangerous." Colin paused again. "On the flip side, since he shot and killed a US marshal and put a sheriff in the hospital, every single agency in law enforcement has eyes out for him right now. I'd put money on the fact that they want him as much as we do."

"Impossible," she said low, almost under her breath.

Colin didn't respond and for a second she thought that maybe he hadn't heard her.

"Agreed," he finally said, almost as quietly.

"He's smart and he has sophisticated channels to hide in," she said. "He's made it this far and he won't stop until I'm six feet underground and he has Angelina."

"First, he has to find you. Then, he has to

plan his attack if he wants to get out alive and/ or without spending the rest of his life behind bars," Colin offered. "Over my dead body he'll take my daughter away."

The words sat thickly in between them.

"I'm betting that he wants it all. Revenge and freedom. And I intend to complicate his plans even further. He'll have to get past me in order to get to either one of you," Colin said after a thoughtful pause.

"I hope you're right about him because that would give us more time. He's intelligent and can be very charismatic but his temper is his weakness. He believes that I wronged him when I betrayed him with the federal government and he'll want me to pay for that more than he wants to breathe. I've heard him say that he won't go back to prison," she said. How many times had he promised her that he'd kill their daughter in front of her eyes if she so much as spoke poorly of him to someone else? What she'd done to him was his worst nightmare come to life.

"A man who can't control his anger will make mistakes. He'll get too focused on revenge and miss an angle," Colin said. "That's where we capitalize."

"There was a man who'd lied to Richard about skimming money off the books," she said. "A week later that same man was found burned alive in his own home. His wife was bound to a chair secured to a wall post. If her mother hadn't been scheduled to come over for lunch the woman would've burned down with the house after watching her husband die."

"Did they have kids?" he asked.

"Three," she supplied. "They'd already left for school."

"Then, the wife must've been involved in the scam somehow," he said after a thoughtful pause.

"What do we do? Run forever trying to get away from him?" she asked, tamping down a wave of panic.

"I can't risk taking him on with you and Angelina here," he said. "For now, I keep you guys out of sight long enough for law enforcement to catch him. They will if we give them a chance."

"You don't think he'll get to my father?" she asked.

"Where is he?" Colin kept his gaze trained on the houseboat.

"All I've been told is that he's in a facility in the Pacific Northwest. That might not even be true." She rocked back and forth. "What if

Richard figures it out and goes after my father to get to me?"

"We'll deal with it," Colin said. She wondered if he'd feel the same if he knew that her father was the reason she was in this situation.

"Maybe we should go there and pick him up to be safe," she said.

"Not a good idea," he quickly countered. "If you knew the name of the facility, I could send someone. But keep in mind he's in protective custody and they've most likely changed his name and location in anticipation of Richard finding the information from Marshal Davis."

He had a good point.

"There's no way for me to check in with the marshal's office, is there?" she asked.

"We need to stay focused on keeping you and Angelina safe," he said. "I'm sure they're doing everything in their power to keep your father protected and that's not who Richard wants anyway."

"He might use him to get to me," she said. "Or he could believe that my father was somehow involved in my decision to help the authorities."

Colin didn't immediately answer. "Those two were in business together, right?"

"Yes. My father got into trouble and Richard partnered with him to help out," she said.

"How?" Colin asked.

"Dad had a gambling problem and eventually it got so bad that he drained his company's cash. To keep business afloat, he started offering an investment opportunity to his suppliers," she said. Her dad had owned a successful auto repair business. "To keep them happy, he paid dividends using the money he'd get from new investors."

"He was running a Ponzi scheme?" he asked.

"Yes," she said. "Needless to say, it ballooned and he ended up in trouble."

"And Richard was there to help him out?" Colin asked.

She nodded. "Richard is smart. He figured out pretty quickly that I'd be willing to do most anything for my family."

Colin's jaw clenched and she suspected he was about to ask her something that she wasn't prepared to answer, like if that was the real reason she left him.

"The best thing you can do right now is keep a positive attitude. I know that can be difficult—"

"Try impossible," she said, thankful he'd moved on instead of pushing her.

"It's important, though. If we panic or lose focus a door will be cracked open for Richard to take advantage of," he said and, once again, he was making sense. "We can't afford to give him anything to work with. For now, we need to set our personal feelings aside."

"You're right." She said a little protection prayer for her father that she'd learned as a child. "I'll try not to dwell on what could happen."

"Good. We'll face what we have in front of us right now and deal with the rest as it comes, okay?" He glanced at her and she realized that statement covered so much more than hiding from Richard.

"I can deal with that," she said.

"I need to know more about Richard. What's important to him?" Colin asked.

"The first thing that comes to mind is his family. His mother probably sits at the top of that list. He puts her on a pedestal," she said, raising her flat palm high above her head. "I think she was suspicious of Angelina's birth. I mean, anyone who could do math and knew anything about pregnancy would have to have questions."

"Did Richard ever attempt the calculations?" he asked.

"He never went to doctor appointments or sonograms. I lied about the due date. Said she was born a month early," she said, remembering how much she'd wished that Colin could have been there.

"What about the birth?" he asked. "Surely the doctors would've given you away."

"I said that I wanted a home birth," she said. "I knew full well that he wouldn't have the stomach for that. He had no problem ordering the end of a man's life but he couldn't handle my morning sickness."

"What about his mother?" he asked.

"If she had questions she kept them to herself," she said. "I'm sure that she would've had suspicions in a few years. Angelina looks more and more like you every day."

"If his mother is important to him, we start with her." Colin stared at the waves battering against the shore. Winds had picked up and the spring thunderstorm was rolling in as promised. Some of the worst storms came late in the season after a cold winter. And this one had been freezing. Warm air clashed with frigid temperatures, causing all kinds of destruction where they met.

"She'll have protection around her 24/7," Melissa said as her hair whipped around her face, the intensity of the threatening storm growing.

"Is she in the family business?" Colin didn't budge. Not even when the first large droplets of rain splattered around them.

Before Melissa could respond, he launched toward her.

Chapter Nine

Melissa reacted quickly, rolling just out of Colin's reach. *Good.*

"Your reflexes are honed. I don't think I want to know why you automatically flinch when a man comes toward you, but I can work with your instincts," he said, lying chest down on the dirt.

Melissa threw a punch at him. He caught her fist in his hand.

"You're not fast enough to pull that off," he said. "We have to learn to work with what you've got."

"I thought we were using strategy to avoid confrontation," she said, staring at her hand.

Did she feel the same jolt of electricity pulsing through her hand and down her arm that he did? Colin didn't want to feel anything when he was around Melissa. "We are. And when that fails, you need to learn how to defend yourself long enough for help to arrive or to get away."

"You asked about his mother earlier. No, she's not in the family business, but that doesn't mean she's stupid to it. It's my observation that she accepts what they do and benefits from the lifestyle she gets out of it. It had never crossed my mind to enjoy a fortune that had been built on other people's blood as much as it had been built on criminal activity, but she didn't seem to mind." Melissa ran her finger along the dirt. "She has a driver, who is always with her. He wouldn't hesitate to shoot first and ask questions later."

"What about security at the family home?" he asked.

"It's rigged with a security system. I was never given the access code to his parents' house. There are dogs. It's probably not as good as the ranch but it would be hard to walk onto the property unnoticed," she said. "Someone's on foot at all times. I don't see guns but I'm sure the men are carrying."

"That could work to our benefit. If the weapons aren't visible then they'll be harder to reach. A few seconds could give us the advantage we need," he said.

"I can't go anywhere near the place without people knowing who I am," she said. "And I'm

praying that you won't leave me and Angelina
alone to fend for ourselves."

Melissa had brought up a good point. He
couldn't exactly stash her and the baby somewhere while he walked into harm's way. He
didn't know Richard well enough to be able
to do proper risk analysis. The assignment to
keep her and Angelina safe while the feds did
their job was going to be challenging enough.

He needed to test her reflexes again now that
she seemed relaxed.

Colin dove to his right.

Melissa flinched and then drew back but
wasn't fast enough.

He was on top of her in a half second, pin-
ning her to the ground. This wasn't the time to
notice how good her body felt pressed against
his. The outside of her legs were being secured
by his thighs and warmth shot through him at
the contact.

Out of nowhere a thunderclap of need
caused his body to vibrate. He shut out the
images of being in this position with her, her
legs wrapped around his waist as he buried
himself deep inside her.

The shock of that deep-seeded desire knocked
him off balance enough for her to push him off
her. He didn't resist because he'd been so caught
off guard that he didn't know what to do with

it. He wanted to keep on resenting her for what she'd done to him. He sure as hell didn't want to feel that same old fire that had been incredible while it burned bright and had threatened to consume him in its shadow.

"Colin, are you okay?" Her voice broke through the raging thoughts in his head.

"Yeah, of course." He finally looked up to see her leaning over him, her brows knitted in concern.

"What happened a minute ago?" she asked. "It's like you mentally checked out."

"It was nothing. That's enough for one day." He forced himself upright. Rain had started coming down faster and they needed to get inside the boat. "Time to get ready to bunk down for the night."

Melissa visibly shook. She'd always been scared of being near water. Colin didn't like putting her in this position any more than he liked the bigger situation they faced. He hoped she could take it. Plan B was to sleep in the truck but they'd get better quality rest inside the houseboat, so that was his first choice. And especially since Richard liked to exploit people's weaknesses. Anger burned inside Colin at what Melissa had had to put up with being with Richard.

Even though it had been her decision to pick

Richard over him—and he'd licked plenty of wounds over her choice—he wasn't the kind of person who'd wish the life she'd signed up for on his worst enemy, and especially not on someone who'd meant so much to him at one point in his life. He refused to allow himself to think there could be any more to his feelings than that. And he sure as hell didn't want to think about what had happened back there on the shoreline as he helped her onto the boat.

"You can have first dibs on the shower," he said to Melissa. "I can keep an eye on the little bug."

She checked on her daughter. *Their daughter.*

"I'll just be a minute," she said, holding on to the counter so tightly that her knuckles turned white.

He and Melissa had a lot to talk about in the very near future. For now, all he could allow himself to think about was Richard.

Colin steered away from the slip and watched out the window as he navigated the boat to Buckner Cove. Lightning flashed sideways across the night sky. The tat-tat-tat of rain on the upstairs deck filled the room.

Colin idled the engine, doing his level best not to think about the fact that Melissa was naked in the shower not twenty away feet from him. He dropped anchor, shut off the engine and pocketed the key.

The houseboat was a rental so there were no clothes he could borrow on board. He'd have to hand wash his own in the sink and let them dry.

He rinsed out the basin and filled it with soapy water. Then he moved to the bathroom and knocked on the door.

"I need your clothes," he said.

"They're on the counter," came the shaky response.

Colin cracked the door open. His body reacted to the silhouette in the shower. He diverted his eyes before his imagination took over, focusing instead on the pile of clothes on the counter.

"Got 'em," he said, anxious to close the door.

Washing Melissa's pale purple silk panties by hand wasn't at the top of Colin's list of things he'd wanted to do today, but they needed clean clothes. He rinsed out her undergarments before placing a towel on the back of the sofa and laying them out to dry. Her blouse and jeans were next.

By the time she emerged from the bathroom, his clothes were clean, hanging to dry, and he was wrapped in a towel waiting his turn. Angelina was still sleeping. The gentle sway of the boat seemed to rock her into a deep slumber.

He was grateful for dim lights. He didn't want to see every detail of her body. As it was, he could see that the beige towel wrapped around her fell mid-thigh. Her long, silky legs were exposed.

"Your turn," she said, gripping the top of her towel like she was dangling from a ledge and the piece of cloth was the only thing between her and dropping to a certain death.

He grunted as he walked past, ignoring all the impulses firing in his body that told him to take her in his arms.

Once inside the shower, he blasted cold water and stood under the spout. His body might want what his brain knew better than to desire but that wouldn't stop him from cooling his jets. He wasn't a reckless kid anymore, and since he'd been old enough to drive a tractor he'd stopped thinking about casual sex. Good sex was another story altogether. He was up for that pretty much anytime. But he was also old enough to know that if he put his hand directly into a fire he'd get burned.

He'd done that once already.

After talking to Melissa about Richard, another picture was starting to emerge. It was probably just Colin's ego talking, but he wondered whether or not leaving him had been her choice. Had Richard done something to her? Threatened her? What could he possibly have over Melissa that would make her walk away from the life they'd planned? He already knew about her father but was there something else? Colin believed, at the time at least, that she'd wanted marriage and a family with him as much as he'd wanted those things with her.

Was he blinded to the reality that someone could swoop in and offer her more? That she could run toward more security?

All her words from a year ago wound through his thoughts…*I don't love you anymore. Not the way that I did when we first met. There's someone else.*

Once the writing was on the wall and she was determined to leave him, he'd closed off his emotions. What they'd had between them had been genuine and real. Or at least that's what he'd believed. What a lovesick fool he'd been. If their feelings had been genuine and equal on both sides—necessary for a shot at a good marriage—she wouldn't have been able to walk away so easily.

Thinking back, it had all happened so fast. Literally, the change in her had been like someone had flipped a switch. Colin remembered being the happiest he'd ever been with his whole life planned out with the woman he loved. He'd been so convinced that she'd been *the one.* And then, like a curveball slamming him in the face while he batted air, his entire world had been tilted on its axis and he had an empty hole in his chest. He'd been left with the burning question…how did he not see this coming?

Part of him wanted to step out of the shower and demand answers. The other part wanted to hurt her in return, let her see how it felt to have her world pulled out from underneath her in the blink of an eye. He was too much of a man to go that route. And he could see that had already happened to her even if he didn't understand the whole situation yet.

He finished his shower and dried off before wrapping the towel around his waist and returning to the other room.

Her gaze flickered across his bare chest and then she quickly turned to face the other direction.

"What's wrong? Afraid you'll offend your husband by seeing another man with his shirt off?" he asked, his anger having returned. It was a low blow but he'd been wallowing in self-pity in the shower. *Damn it, O'Brien.* He was a better man than that.

Before he could apologize, she whirled around on him.

"You want me to look at you?" she asked, all fire and sass. "You want me to admit that I missed you? Fine. I did, Colin. I missed you and I'm sorry that I hurt you, but the past year hasn't exactly been a picnic for me, either, so if you want to hurt me even more just know that you can't."

He was close enough to see the tears streaming down her cheeks.

Ah, hell. He hadn't meant to cause that.

"You want to know what my life was like?" she pushed. "Do you *really want to know*?"

He opened his mouth to apologize but she shut him down again.

"Imagine the worst day you've ever had… the day you found out your parents were… *gone*…imagine waking up every day and *that* moment replaying over and over again. That moment being your life." Her eyes were wild and he'd never seen her like this before. "And then imagine that whoever did that to them was after someone else you loved and there was nothing you could do to stop it. People were getting hurt all around you and you had no power to stop it."

"Tell me what he did to you, Melissa," he said. He needed to hear the words.

"If it would change anything, I'd be all for it," she said. "Right now, all I can think about is staying alive so that I can take care of my little girl. I get that you hate me. I hurt you and I probably deserve whatever anger you whirl at me. But my life has been hell and I just want this nightmare to end. Nothing else matters until it does."

Colin wasn't normally at a loss for words. Standing there in the kitchen, her body vibrating from anger, he couldn't think of one positive thing to say to calm her down. His own body was chorded with tension, strung so tight he thought his muscles might snap, so he threw all rationale to the wind, pulled her into his arms and kissed her.

Her muscles tensed against him and he half figured she'd pull away and throw a punch like she had on the shore. Instead, she leaned into him and popped up onto her tiptoes to deepen the kiss. Colin groaned against her mouth and then pulled back.

All he'd hoped to do was calm her down, not stir up a bunch of...*feelings*. That kiss was like a shotgun blast to the chest and stirred up an inappropriate reaction down south. He took a step back, put his hands behind him and gripped the edge of the counter to keep from doing any further damage. The thought that both of them were naked underneath their towels wasn't the one he wanted to have.

"That shouldn't have happened," Melissa said.

"Agreed."

"It won't happen again," she continued.

He crossed his arms over his chest and smirked. "Well, it shouldn't."

She laughed and it was the first real break in tension since seeing her again. Thunder cracked and she flinched. It was the same reaction she'd had to him making a move toward her on the bank. Another second ticked by and she recovered.

He wanted to ask her what that was all about but figured better of it.

"Now what do we do?" she asked, diverting her eyes from whatever she'd been staring at on his chest.

Colin located the throwaway phone and then held it up on the flat palm of his right hand. "First, we check on Tommy."

"Can we do that without giving away our location?" she asked.

"Yes." He held up his hand and nodded. He called the main number to Bluff General, a number he'd committed to memory when his parents had been admitted, a number he didn't want to have to know.

"Can you connect me to a volunteer on the second floor?" he asked when the operator answered.

"Yes, sir," the calm, pleasant and practiced female voice on the other end of the line said.

After a few seconds of elevator music, a chipper voice chimed in. "This is Renee. How may I help you?"

"I'm wondering if you can do me a huge favor," he said.

"Okay." Renee sounded excited.

Good.

"In Room 207 will be a visitor named Mr. O'Brien. If you could ask him if the package I sent made it to its destination, I'd sure be able to sleep a whole lot better tonight," he said. He didn't need to know which brother was in the room but he knew for certain one of them would be there. Giving the last name would cut down on any confusion because any of his brothers would be able to figure out the cryptic message.

"Who should I tell him wants to know?" she asked, ever perky.

"This is Cardin from Dan's Delivery Service," he said. All of his brothers would remember the nickname one of the twins gave him when they were little. Two-year-old Joshua

had said *Cardin* instead of *Colin* and it had
stuck for a few years.

"Okay, sir. Would you mind holding?" she
asked.

"Not at all," Colin said.

It took a full five minutes for her to return.

"I'm sorry, sir. The room is empty."

Chapter Ten

"What do you mean the room's empty?" Colin asked. Those last three words echoed in Melissa's head as all the air was sucked out of the room in a whoosh.

News like that couldn't be good. Tommy was stable last night. He'd been moved to a recovery area.

Melissa centered herself by gripping the edge of the table.

"Has the patient been moved?" he asked, and then she heard him give Tommy's name.

The silence sent cold chills down Melissa's spine.

"Can you check at the nurse's stand?" he asked, his gaze intensely focused on a spot on the floor. "Yes, I'll hold."

Melissa moved next to Colin and then he tilted the earpiece so that she could hear.

"The patient was moved. I'm not authorized

to give his room number but you'll be happy to know that your package arrived safely and all is well. We paged Mr. O'Brien and he confirmed receipt," she said with a self-satisfied tone.

"Thanks, Renee. It means a lot to have that confirmed," he said, and Melissa could hear the relief in his voice.

"You betcha. Anything else I can help with tonight?" she chirped.

"That's it for tonight," he said before wishing her a good evening and ending the call.

A flash of light was followed by a brilliant thunderclap that felt like it was directly on top of them.

Melissa flinched at the same time she gasped.

Colin looked at her and his gaze sent goose bumps up her arms—goose bumps that were totally inappropriate under the circumstances. Then again, so was that kiss, and she couldn't stop thinking about it.

"It's late and you should probably try to get some rest," he said.

Melissa released a deep breath. Relief was quickly replaced by anger. Richard had put her in this position in the first place. He'd tortured her for twelve long months. It was time to make it stop. She turned to face Colin. There wasn't more than a foot between them and she could see his pulse pound at the base of his throat no matter how calm his facade remained.

"What are we going to do to find that jerk?" she asked.

"We're not." Colin's shoulders were tense, belying his casual words.

"I know what you said about staying hidden until they catch him, but how long is that going to take?" she asked. "How much longer do I have to wait?"

"Good question," he said. "One I don't have an answer to."

"We can't just stay here and hide. He'll find us eventually," she said, hoping she was getting through.

"You're frustrated and I get that, but we have another priority right now." He stared at the bassinet. "I want to go after the guy more than—"

She shot him a look that said, "Impossible."

He put up a hand. "Okay, as much as you do. But we made the decision to keep Angelina with us and as long as she's here, we can't risk a direct approach."

Colin was making perfect sense and yet she wasn't ready to concede. Her body was chorded with tension and there'd be no break until Richard was behind bars.

"It's only been one day," Colin reasoned.

Again, he was making sense that she wasn't quite ready to accept. "We have to give it a little more time, Melissa."

He'd made good points. The farther Angelina was from Richard, the safer she'd be. Obviously, her daughter was her first priority.

"I'm just so angry and frustrated," she said.

Colin launched toward her.

She ducked but not in time. His arms closed around her midsection and all kinds of unwanted sensations trilled through her body.

He pinned her against the counter with his large frame.

"You need to be ready at all times. When you let your emotions run wild, you lose focus," he said, and his voice was a deep growl that poured over her.

With his body flush with hers, his muscled chest against her breasts, it was impossible to think.

And then the rain pattering on the rooftop seemed to stop. The world felt as though it stopped spinning as everything stilled. All Melissa could hear was her heart pounding inside her chest. All she could feel was the heat and electricity pinging between the two of them. All she wanted to do was reach up and kiss Colin again.

Pupils large, lips compressed, he appeared

to be as surprised by the instant change in chemistry as she'd been.

"You take the bed. I'll bunk down for the night on the couch," he said after a long pause.

COLIN LAY ON the couch, facing the ceiling. Thunder cracked in the sky overhead and he half expected Melissa to bolt through the door or the baby to wake. Neither budged. He flipped onto his side. The thin blanket covering him slipped off and landed on the floor. He picked up the tan piece of cotton and repositioned, trying to get comfortable. The material wasn't much bigger than the bath towel Melissa had been wearing earlier. Sleep was about as realistic as an ice storm in a Texas summer.

He sat up. Something was bothering him and he couldn't quite pinpoint what it was. Melissa wasn't telling him everything. It was clear that she was afraid of her husband—correction, her soon-to-be ex. And there was something else niggling at the back of his mind.

Obviously Rancic was a ruthless criminal. Figuring out how to find him wasn't as cut-and-dried, especially with Angelina in the picture. Taking care of a three-month-old was already a full-time job—forget trying to track down a criminal while keeping the baby out of harm's way.

Colin peeked inside the bassinet. The thought that he and Melissa had a daughter together sent his mind into a tailspin. At one time, this had been the plan. And then, like a tornado touching down, everything had changed. He'd done his best to move on in the past twelve months. Events of the past twenty-four hours already had his mind whirling.

He had questions, not the least of which was why she'd married Richard in the first place. It was becoming obvious there was so much more to the story, especially given how afraid she was of the guy. Colin told himself that the only reason he cared was because his daughter was involved and it had nothing to do with the feelings resurfacing for Melissa.

His daughter. Those two words would take getting used to. Angelina wasn't the problem. That little thing with big brown eyes and just enough curly black hair on her head to make her adorable was an angel. To be fair, he'd believed her to be a cutie even before he realized she belonged to him.

Colin had grown up around brothers. He had five of his own: Dallas, Austin, Tyler, and the twins, Ryder and Joshua. Then, there was Tommy. He'd grown up on the ranch as one of the boys. Colin didn't have the first idea what to do with a girl. He'd figure it out, though.

First, he'd deal with Rancic.

As far as figuring out the future, Colin hadn't given himself time to think about more than the next hour or two. One thing was certain. That precious girl deserved to have two parents with their acts together.

Another bolt of lightning lit up the room. A loud *crack* sounded.

This time, Angelina stirred. Colin moved even closer to her, standing over her bassinet. It was one thing to be handed a baby from someone else. How the heck did he pick her up without hurting her?

Her big eyes opened and she blinked up at him. Her whimper nearly cracked his heart in half.

There was no sign of Melissa and he had no idea how to fix the formula. He didn't want his little girl crying any longer than she had to.

After a couple of aborted attempts, he finally secured her head with one hand as he bent down close enough to lift her to his chest with the other. She was wiggly and felt a little too loose in his hands. His heart squeezed at the thought of even the slightest possibility of dropping her. There was no way he would allow that to happen. He hugged her firmly and bounced up and down.

The boat was already rocking them from

side to side, making Colin unsure about his footing. He didn't like that. Angelina was winding up for what promised to be a loud cry based on his limited experience with her so far. He took a few steps toward the bedroom pocket door that was closed.

Angelina's cries were heartbreaking. As much as he wanted to leave Melissa alone, he realized that he couldn't do this without her.

"I know you're hungry. Let's go wake up your mom," Colin soothed, wishing he was further along on the learning curve of taking care of his daughter.

He made it halfway to the door when it opened.

"Sick," she said. Melissa's face was white. On closer inspection, maybe a little green. She looked torn between taking her crying baby in her arms and being afraid she might throw up on her.

"Tell me what to do," he said.

"She likes singing," she said.

"Tell me something else to do. My singing will make her cry even more," he said, bouncing as gently as he could.

"A bottle." Melissa's hand came up. She covered her mouth. The weather wasn't cooperating. It had the boat rocking back and forth.

"Trash can's under the sink," he said.

She held on to the wall to keep her balance as she moved. He followed her. Everything he needed for the baby was in the diaper bag and the kitchen, and he wanted to make sure that Melissa was okay.

The waves were big enough outside to make moving around on the boat a challenge. Navigating out of the cove in this weather wasn't a good option, either. They needed to stay the course. His only solace was Rancic was nowhere around. Keeping Angelina and Melissa safe was his first priority.

Melissa was getting sick in the bathroom. The baby was crying. The storm raged outside. It seemed intent on not giving them a break.

"I'm sorry," Melissa managed to say in between heaves.

"You're doing fine" he said calmly. She needed reassurance as much as Angelina needed her bottle. Both were urgent and he needed to be the calm in the storm for both of them.

"There's a formula packet in the diaper bag. First, you put the plastic liner in the bottle and then add the powder," she said. "I'll heat water in the microwave."

She worked quickly in between heaves.

Colin somehow managed to get the liner inside the plastic bottle and the packet of powder where it needed to go. That he managed to pull any of it off without spilling a speck of powder was nothing short of a miracle.

"How can you possibly be smiling?" Melissa asked and she broke into a smile, too, as she helped finish up the bottle.

He just shook his head and kept on grinning.

Angelina immediately settled down as soon as she started sucking on the nipple and the warm milk passed her lips.

"Hearing her cry is the worst," Colin said, situating himself on a chair in the kitchen so he could hold his daughter more comfortably without fear of dropping her.

"Believe me, I know," she said. "She sounds so pitiful."

He nodded.

"The first few weeks were awful. She'd cry and I didn't have the first idea how to handle it. I just wanted to comfort her but I felt like I was doing everything wrong. Then, I don't know, I guess I started getting more confident with being a mother," she said.

Melissa had been an only child and didn't grow up close to cousins. Colin knew that it had just been her, and she'd often commented about how lucky he'd been to have so many brothers around. Of course, he'd joke about how messy the bathroom had been but he wouldn't change his childhood for the world. Yeah, his family had money and they hadn't wanted for anything. But Dad had built his fortune from the ground up and had never forgotten his roots. And maybe that's why their family fortune was nothing but zeroes in a bank account to Colin. Looking at her now, he wondered if he'd placed more emphasis on giving her material things if she would've left him for Richard in the first place.

It was the pain talking. He chalked it up to wounded pride. In his heart he realized that he'd never want to be with a person who cared more about his bank account than building a real life with him. Money was important, don't get him wrong, but it didn't guarantee a person's happiness. Aunt Bea and Uncle Ezra were prime examples. Dad had given them both a small piece of his business so that they'd be taken care of in their later years and yet all the two of them ever did was argue. Money couldn't bring his parents back. Or give him more time with the people he loved. But he was also realizing that money was only part of the reason Melissa had left. She hadn't trusted him enough to tell him what was going on.

"You look much better," he said. Her color was returning and her cheeks were flushed.

She rinsed her mouth out and then splashed

water on her face. "It's been a crazy few days, hasn't it?"

"Nothing we can't deal with," he said.

"So what made you smile before?" she asked.

"All of this. Being on a boat in a storm with you. The fact that I have a daughter," he said. "I guess this scenario amused me. This is pretty much the last place on earth I expected to be and the situation we're in is even more bizarre. I'm not exactly one to run the other way from trouble."

"No, you're not," she agreed.

"When she was crying a few minutes ago, I'd never felt so helpless in my life," he admitted. "She seems so little, so fragile."

"I felt the same way when I first held her," Melissa said, and she had a wistful look in her eyes. "I was pretty sure that I was going to mess up the whole parenting thing. Not being able to breastfeed was a big blow in that department. But then I started slowly figuring things out and we started to get into a routine. I think she likes a schedule, actually."

Colin glanced down. The liner was almost empty. "She was hungry."

"You should stop before she sucks air. It'll make her tummy hurt," Melissa said.

He gently pulled the bottle out of his daughter's mouth. Being able to feed her and give her what she needed brought on a surprising bout of emotions. It felt good.

"We should get her burped and changed, and then we'll be good for another four hours or so. Sometimes I get five or six," Melissa said, walking toward him. He handed over the baby and watched as Melissa placed their daughter against her right shoulder. She patted the little girl's back until she made a few gurgling noises and then belched.

"She has strong lungs. There's no doubt about that," Colin said as he followed Melissa into the next room.

"Can you bring a diaper and the package of wipes?" Melissa positioned their daughter as he grabbed supplies. Angelina was sound asleep and didn't stir.

He handed the items to her and watched her fluid movements as she changed the baby's diaper. There was something so natural about being with Melissa again. Seeing how much she loved their daughter. It had to be a sign that she'd given their daughter the name they'd picked out. Those thoughts confused the hell out of him when he considered what she'd done to him.

"I hear the moms on the ranch say the same thing about having their babies on a routine," he offered, trying to give some reassurance.

"She's doing really well considering the fact that our world has been turned upside down in a second," Melissa said.

Was she regretting turning over evidence on Rancic? Colin's defenses kicked in.

"Did you mean being on the run from your husband?" he asked, and she shot him a look when he said the last word. It was true. She was married to Richard.

"I wish you'd stop reminding me of that," she said under her breath. She placed the baby in the bassinet and stalked out of the room.

Chapter Eleven

By the time the sun came up, Colin needed a strong cup of black coffee more than he needed air. There was no way he was going to leave Melissa or the baby alone to get one, though.

He woke with the last words spoken between him and Melissa fresh on his mind. Seeing her and the baby together, knowing Angelina was his, threatened to chip away at his armor and leave him exposed. The two looked so natural together and they felt like his family.

Colin couldn't believe his own stupidity. He'd started tripping down the road that could only lead to disaster with Melissa. He mentally slapped himself for momentarily forgetting just how burned he'd been before.

Don't get too comfortable, O'Brien.

Darkness loomed on the horizon and Colin needed to focus all his attention on keeping his daughter and Melissa safe.

At least the storm had abated, if only for a little while. He'd checked the weather and it was supposed to be even worse that evening. Melissa had barely made it through last night. There was no way she'd survive worse. With severe lightning in the forecast, he didn't want to take a chance and stay on the boat. He'd have to scout a better location before the next round of storms rolled in.

Being on the run with a three-month-old wasn't exactly an ideal scenario. He'd thought about it all night and Melissa had had a point. They couldn't hide forever. Richard or one of his men would catch up to them sooner or later, and they were vulnerable while traveling with the baby. Colin couldn't even contemplate going after the man while Angelina was with them. They were stuck between a place of needing to protect their daughter and stopping the threat.

He stared at the dark-haired angel happily sleeping in her bassinet. The fact that he was a father was starting to sink in. There was no doubt that he'd do everything he could for his daughter. For a flicker, he thought about asking Melissa for custody, but he couldn't see her going for that after watching their bond last night. She wasn't an unfit mother. In fact, when he'd watched her feed the baby again at the crack of dawn, he'd been awed at how much she loved that little girl. She sang a soothing song and he'd pretended to be asleep to give them privacy.

Awe was great, but there was no way he was confusing that for real feelings between him and Melissa. As far as Colin was concerned, that ship had sailed. He needed to remind himself of the fact often because it was all too easy to forget when he saw her with his daughter.

The door to the bedroom opened at first light and Melissa walked into the room looking like she'd had about as good a night's sleep as he did.

"Storm passed," he said. In daylight he could really see the dark circles cradling her eyes.

"Yeah, about an hour ago," she said. Even though she walked like a zombie, she looked good. He tried not to think about the pale purple undergarments he'd washed yesterday— the ones she was wearing—as she checked on the baby.

"I figure I'll go into town for supplies early before folks are up and moving. Pick up some coffee," he said.

She plopped down on the couch next to him. It didn't help that when he'd tried to sleep there'd been a metal rod beneath the too-thin cushion that had poked his back all night.

"You didn't get any rest, did you?" she asked. "I can tell when you're tired. Your voice gets deep and your eyes are even darker."

"Don't need much sleep to function," he said, telling himself that he didn't care how well she knew him. "I got enough to do what needs to be done today. That's all that matters."

"Military training kicking in again?" she asked.

He nodded again and then rubbed the scruff on his chin.

"Coffee sounds like heaven right now," she said. "Did you check the cupboard to see if there was any?"

"At about four o'clock this morning," he said. "We can head out whenever you're ready."

"Just let me brush my teeth and wash my face," she said, pushing off the couch. "Then I'll need to wake Angelina, of course. She fed a little while ago so she won't need to eat again for a few hours. We're good there."

Colin had already brushed his teeth and was ready to go. His muscles were sore from the uncomfortable position he'd been in during the night. He moved to the hallway, took off his shirt and set it on the bench seat in the dining room. He dropped down for a few morning push-ups to get the blood pumping. There was someone in the next room who got other parts of him stirring by walking into a room.

Colin didn't need to think about her right now.

WAKING TO SEE shirtless Colin holding their daughter against his chest last night, sick or not, made Melissa's heart free-fall. They'd had a few good moments before he'd armored up again. She could understand if he couldn't have feelings for her anymore but she hoped that one day he'd be able to forgive her.

When her father had come to her with the proposal for her to marry Richard in order to get him out of a bad business deal, she'd laughed. In her mind, there was no way he could be serious. But then he'd sat her down at the table and fixed a pot of coffee. That was the routine saved for grave moments, like when he'd told her that her mother had gone to heaven and wasn't coming back. That the two of them were a team now.

Melissa's heart pounded against her chest just thinking about it.

Her father had poured two cups and set one down in front of her. He'd taken the seat across the table before clasping his hands and resting his elbows on the table.

"This is serious," he'd said with that same

ominous tone he'd used on the warm summer morning, too low and too calm.

Melissa's chest had squeezed as she'd tried to force herself to breathe.

"I'm in trouble and I could go away for a long time if word gets out. Richard has offered an escape route." Her father's face had looked so anguished. "I think we should take it."

Thinking about her own daughter, the strong need to protect her above all else, Melissa couldn't fathom taking away that choice for her. Because once it was out there that Richard was the only salvation, that it was about more than just getting the money to pay Richard back, she would have no other choice but to agree. Her father had been the first to say that he'd gladly swallow his pride and ask the O'Briens for help if that were the case. Colin had plenty of money even if Melissa didn't and they were known for being a generous family.

Maybe Melissa could've gone to her fiancé for help. Part of her never really could completely trust a man after some of her father's actions over the years. Another part didn't have the heart to go to Colin. Would it have been embarrassing? Yes. But she trusted their relationship enough to realize that Colin would've done what it took to bail out her father. But

Richard had evidence against her father that would send him to jail.

Could she have talked to Colin? The problem was that he would've sought revenge if he'd known that it hadn't been her choice to leave. He would've kept coming back, and her heart couldn't take seeing him once she'd agreed to marry Richard. And in order to keep her father from going to jail, she'd had to marry Richard.

When she'd gotten cold feet at the last minute and said she needed more time, Richard's brother had visited her. He'd made it clear that no one hurt his family. And then there was the threat to Colin's family.

Her heart thudded.

Everything had happened so fast. In hindsight, she might've handled things differently. But she'd done the best she could under the circumstances.

"I've been thinking about a few possibilities to bring the fight to Richard's doorstep. I keep coming around to one. We have to pull him out of hiding and get him back in the area. We have to—"

Melissa held her hand up. Richard could still play his card against the O'Brien family and they needed to be prepared.

"Before we go down this road any further, I need to tell you something, Colin." She left no room for doubt with the seriousness of those words. A lump was forming in her throat and she didn't want to be the one to tell him this news—news that could shatter him.

Colin motioned toward the small kitchen table with a three-sided bench seat, the back of which was attached to the wall. Talking to him while she wore an oversized T-shirt with the word *Bahamas* plastered across the front made her so much more aware of how vulnerable she felt being close to him.

"Give me a minute to get dressed and then we'll talk," she said. Was a part of her stalling for time? Probably. She'd need a minute to gather her resolve. Colin needed to hear this from her, not read it in the papers or be ambushed by the news or however Richard deemed appropriate to deliver it.

"Your clothes are still damp," he warned.

"I don't care." She gathered her garments and took them into the bedroom. She returned a few minutes later feeling more like she could handle what she needed to say. She knew how much he loved his parents, and hearing something like this after losing them would be a hard blow. But she'd rather be the one to tell him because if he planned to draw Richard out, then he needed to know exactly what weapons the man had in his arsenal. Information could be just as damaging as a knife.

She took a seat across from Colin, noticing that he'd put on his jeans. Maybe he'd picked up on her discomfort at being scarcely covered.

"I don't know how he knew this or why, but Richard will come after your family with something very damaging," she began, twisting her fingers together as she spoke.

"There's nothing he can do to hurt my family. The ranch is secure," he said, but she untangled her fingers and held a hand up to stop him. He needed to hear this. From her.

"I'm not saying that he'll physically attack or try to get past security. I know Gideon can handle whatever comes at him in Bluff. I just think that if we're considering going after his family, you should know the way in which he'll come after yours." She was dancing around the topic, stalling as long as she could. She needed to gather her strength. The problem was that she loved his parents. When she'd first heard the news she denied it, not wanting to accept that it could be real. But then he'd shown her the pictures and she couldn't deny it any longer…

"Richard has proof that your father was—" she took in a deep breath and looked him straight in the eye "—having an affair."

"Oh, yeah? What does he think he has?" Colin asked calmly, surprisingly unaffected by the bomb she'd just dropped.

"He had pictures of your father with another woman," she said, and her eyebrow must've risen because Colin smirked. "What?"

"If I had a nickel for every time a random person tried to accuse someone in my family of doing something wrong, I'd be a rich man," he quipped.

"I hate to point out the obvious, but you already are a rich man," she countered.

"I'd be even wealthier," he said, and then took a casual sip of water.

"So, you don't believe me?" Melissa balked.

"Oh, no. I believe you one hundred percent."

"Then fill me in because I'm confused," she said.

"Pictures don't mean anything. There are so many ways to doctor them with computer programs. Surely, you know that," he said.

"Nothing about these looked fake," she said. "I must've checked them a dozen times."

"Did you recognize the woman? We can track her down and ask if it would make you feel better," he said.

"These pictures get out and it'll hurt your family business if not your relationships with each other. This is your parents we're talking about, Colin," she said, not willing to accept that she'd sacrificed the past year and lost the love of her life over potentially fake photos. Obviously, there'd been more to it than that. Richard had been blackmailing her father and threatening him with jail. No matter what else was false, that was true.

But she'd gotten through more than 365 horrible days by reminding herself that she was doing this for Colin's family, as well. It had somehow eased some of the pain of being forced to walk away from him.

Of course, figuring out she was six weeks pregnant two weeks into her marriage had complicated things even further. Richard must've realized she could never have real feelings for him, and why he seemed content with a facade she would never know. Richard was a collector. He liked to buy shiny things and look at them on the shelves in his office. She was never more than another shiny object to him.

"If a couple of pictures could bring down the foundation of our business or our relationships with each other, they weren't strong to begin with." He shrugged it off, but his gaze intensified on her.

She could read between the lines. He was saying that if a little squall like Richard could destroy their relationship, it wasn't much of one.

"That's not true. Houses can be brought down by a ten-minute dust storm and you know it," she said a little too quickly.

"Again, it wasn't much of a house if it could be brought down by a couple of strong winds." He folded his arms across his chest.

It was pretty clear that he wasn't talking about his parents any longer. This conversation was at a standstill.

Her mind was bouncing all over the place, especially in contrast to how calm Colin was being. While he'd been the cool, casual brother for the most part, he'd also had a quick temper and could make snap judgments about situations and people. It was part of the reason she didn't want to drag him into the situation with her father. She'd feared that he'd go off half-cocked and make everything so much worse. It was hard to imagine life could become more complicated than it had.

Colin had changed in the past year. Grown up. He seemed so much more…centered and in control. Don't get her wrong, half the excitement of their relationship had been due to his unpredictable nature. She'd never known what to expect from one day to the next except that she never had to question how much he loved her. That part had been secure.

And they could talk for hours. He was the

only person on earth who really knew her and understood her. His impulsive and unpredictable side had been so much a part of his charm and worked even better at seducing her.

But then that was the past. So much had changed in the last year.

"I guess I was wrong then," she said. "But what makes you so sure he didn't have an affair?"

"If he did, that was between my parents. Neither said anything to us and so I have to trust that they believed what they had was worth fighting for and they worked it out. Here's the thing I can be certain about. They had a strong marriage and that would be impossible to have without total honesty," he said so automatically, so naturally.

She wished she had half his confidence.

"I'm more concerned with why my parents' marriage would even come up in a conversation between you and your...ex," he said, those intense dark eyes staring right into her.

"We had a fight and I threatened to walk out," she said, and that was partially true. "He thought I was still in love with you and said that if I ran back to you he'd destroy your family. I didn't believe that he could so he showed me."

"You threatened to leave him from the beginning?" Colin asked, and she was glad that he left alone the part about her still being in love with him.

"It was early in our marriage," she said. "And like I said, we'd had a fight."

"What was the argument really about?" he asked.

She just stared at him for a long moment. And then she said, "You."

"Why would you and your hus..." he glanced at her with an apologetic look, "*ex* be talking about me at all? You were pretty clear with your feelings when you threw my engagement ring at me and walked out."

Those words were impossible to hear coming out of Colin's mouth. They were like daggers being thrown and it didn't matter how relaxed his tone came across—she knew there was pain on his side, too.

Melissa pushed off the table and walked into the bedroom.

"Hold on a sec," Colin said, trailing after her into the small hallway that lead to the bathroom and bedroom. His hand pressed to her shoulder and suddenly she was being whirled around to face him in the hallway. The space felt small a second ago and even more so now that she was standing there with Colin. His big frame blocked out all the light from the other room. The bedroom door was four steps behind her and the bathroom was to her left. Even though the boat had stopped rocking, it felt like the world tilted with him so close.

And she was trapped between two closed doors, a wall and Colin. Not that it mattered. Where could she go? She was trapped in the middle of a lake with him.

The boat was still but talking about the past, bringing up all those intense feelings she'd had when she'd left Colin, was starting to make her feel sick again. "I need to go. I have to get off here and figure something else out. This isn't working."

Chapter Twelve

Melissa didn't want to look Colin in the face or let him see that she was about to cry.

"Don't run away from me, Melissa," he said. "Not this time."

"Low blow, Colin," she shot back, trying to regain her equilibrium.

"Is it? You keep running and I'm just trying to help you," he said. "You're not telling me everything. I still know you well enough to know that. And that's fine if you don't want to talk to me. I get that there are things between a husband and a wife that other people don't need to know. I can see that you don't trust me. You didn't before and that's most likely why you walked out in the first place."

Melissa sucked in a burst of air.

"You don't think I believed in you?" She fired the words like buckshot. "In us? After everything I've told you? You still don't get it?"

"Don't worry about it. I've learned to deal. It's fine. I'm still going to figure out a way to get to Richard and take him down. I'm still going to figure out a way to make sure you and our daughter are safe from your husband," he said.

"Stop calling him my husband," Melissa barked. Anger and frustration got the best of her and she was shaking. Maybe it was the fact that her nerves were still fried from being on this boat in a storm last night. Wasn't that just her luck? Or maybe it was because she still had the same feelings for Colin that she did a year ago and seeing him, being this close to him but in such a different way, had been eating away at her from the inside out. She knew that they could never have what they'd had before. It was gone. Lost. And so was she except for that little girl not fifteen feet away, sleeping in a bassinet.

Melissa's anger was building and building until all twelve months of frustration boiled over. "He's not my husband. I didn't love him. I never loved him. Got it? And I don't need you to keep telling me how he was my husband because he wasn't. Not in my heart. Not in any way that mattered."

Her heart pounded her ribs and her breath

came out in pulses. Her outburst seemed to silence Colin because he didn't speak a word.

"I don't need you telling me what my relationship was. I certainly don't want to talk about it with you. I can't stand him. He's a criminal and I…" She stopped herself right there. No way was she going to tell him that Richard had done nothing but repulse her.

Colin stood in front of her, contemplating her. His calm demeanor frustrated her even more.

"Move out of the way." She tried to push past him but her hand met a wall.

"It's clear to me that you had no intention of leaving him until the government stepped in. So, why did you name our daughter Angelina?" he asked, those intense eyes of his looking right through her.

And the air *whooshed* from her lungs.

"Because I love that name." It was true. She loved the name and everything it had represented, which boiled down to every day she'd spent with him. There was so much anger in his eyes now. She knew that leaving him would be the hardest thing she'd ever done. Little did she know that she'd had it all wrong. Standing in front of him, facing him, was by far the most difficult.

His expression faltered. "But that was *our*

name. For *our* baby if we ever had a girl. And yet you were content to use it with another man."

"She's your daughter," Melissa quipped.

"He didn't know that and I wouldn't have, either," he said.

Was he trying to hurt her? What did any of it really matter? He'd been clear. He would never trust her again. Their "house" had been made of cards and the first strong wind had blown it down. He'd made excellent points. What did that really say about their relationship?

Melissa couldn't keep going if she opened that dam. She had to stay focused on finding Richard and making him pay for what he'd done to her and so many others.

She folded her arms, needing to get this conversation back on track.

"He was trying to buy a place in Colorado but he didn't want his name on it," she said.

A look of hurt passed behind Colin's steely gaze before he seemed to shore up his resolve, too. "Good. We can start there."

He turned around, his back to her, and walked to the kitchen. Before taking a seat at the table, he rummaged around for a piece of paper and a pen. "Where?"

"Crow's Peak, Colorado. And there's another thing. I know he's made a lot of enemies just in the time I've known him." She was trying hard to think, which was difficult given the fact that water was everywhere, she was on a boat that had rocked all night and had turned her stomach upside down. She was trapped with a man who made her crazy and want things she shouldn't. Her heart was a mess. At least the storm outside had calmed down.

"Let's see. The Colorado deal sticks out the most in my mind. He appeared clean in almost every business deal but blackmail was his specialty. People were too scared to testify against him so he ended up getting whatever he wanted." She couldn't look at Colin when she said those words.

"Who did he blackmail?" he asked, and his voice was a study in calm.

"He tried to keep his business life separate from home for the most part. He never kept a home office. He and his brother, Ray, met at our home sometimes but they kept the volume of the TV turned up. Richard always assumed someone was listening. He was the kind of guy who covered his tracks," she said.

"Did he blackmail you into marrying him?" Colin asked.

Melissa didn't immediately answer.

"What do you mean?" she finally asked.

"You heard my question," he said.

"We're getting off track here," Melissa said.

Colin paused before asking, "Tell me more about the Colorado deal."

"One of his buddies planned to sell the hotel to him and they kept talking about using off-shore accounts and a dummy company." Richard had set up several networks to help other criminals disappear. Any one of the men he'd harbored would help him in a heartbeat if asked.

"It would be a good way to launder money," Colin said. "Isn't that one of his forms of income?"

She nodded. It was one of many illegal activities that Richard managed to keep a hand in.

"Maybe we should start there," Colin said. "I have to say that I don't like the idea of getting close to Richard while we have Angelina with us."

"I agree," she said, her heart rate picking up again. "But I can't be apart from her. I have to be able to protect her, Colin. Especially after being so unsure that I'd be able to for the past year. From the moment I knew I was pregnant I've been a mess thinking about how much he could hurt me using her."

The baby stirred. A little cry sounded in the next room.

"I'll get her," she said quickly.

ANGELINA WAS AWAKE and it was important to keep positive energy between her parents, so he needed to shift gears. Colin was surprised at just how much the new babies on the ranch picked up on. If a situation was tense, they cried or acted out. If everything was calm, they responded with happiness.

"They say the storm is going to be worse tonight," he said. "I'd planned to stay on the boat for a few days. Plans have changed. We'll need dry land."

"Where will we go?" Melissa asked, her gaze darting around, and he could see real fear in her eyes. Talking about Richard brought out intense emotions in her.

"We can figure that out after coffee," he said with a slight smile. Too much conversation had already gone on without caffeine and he needed to dial down his intensity for Angelina's sake. It wasn't easy. But Colin would do anything for that little girl.

"I'll get the baby ready." Melissa had everything ready to go in five minutes, baby in her arms, diaper bag slung over her shoulder.

Colin steered the houseboat back to the bay slowly, making sure there weren't any law enforcement officers waiting for him. After all, he had technically stolen the boat. He parked and then took one of the rental brochures so he could reimburse the family who owned the Sea Fairy. He'd make sure the owners were more than compensated for "lending" their rental.

Melissa had changed. At more than one point during the storms last night he'd expected her to come out of the bedroom for reassurance. Being with Angelina made a difference. There was a sense of determination and purpose to Melissa's personality now. She was protective. The change looked good on her.

Now that Colin could set his emotions aside and think a little more clearly, he was also beginning to piece together a few possibilities of why Melissa might've really left him. He didn't like the scenarios playing out in his head. In fact, they made him want to put his hands on Richard and show him what it really was to be afraid.

From what Colin could gather so far, Melissa had been damn brave. She'd reacted big time to his question about being blackmailed. He had every intention of getting to the bottom of that later when the two of them could focus on something besides nailing Richard.

Colin pulled into the dock and then tied the boat down. He helped Melissa off, ignoring the frissons of heat prickling his hand where it touched hers.

"Mind if I give that a try?" he asked, motioning toward the baby's seat in the back of Dallas's pickup.

A reluctant look passed behind Melissa's eyes before she nodded her head and then handed Angelina over to him.

"Careful," she said as she stood, watching over his shoulder.

Melissa needed to get used to the fact that Angelina's father intended to be around to watch her grow up.

Balancing her head as he lifted her into the seat was going to be the tricky part, he decided.

"Don't worry," he reassured Melissa. "I'm not going to do anything that could possibly hurt our daughter."

"You're right." There was a note of resignation in her voice. She must've taken that wrong. He didn't mean anything by it. He really wouldn't do anything to hurt his daughter on purpose. It was that simple. He'd sort out that miscommunication later when Angelina was safely secured in the car seat. Besides, he had a few rounds of apologies to deliver once this was over. He'd been off since Melissa had returned. Thinking back, he'd practically bit Cynthia's head off at the Spring Fling when he'd found out that Melissa was there.

Colin thought about it. Maybe some of Melissa's actions last year had to do with his immaturity. She hadn't trusted him and that was a problem, especially since they'd planned to spend the rest of their lives together. In hindsight, he could admit that there were situations he could've handled better.

He gently held out Angelina. Balancing her over the seat was nerve-racking. He could only hope that she wouldn't suddenly wiggle at the wrong time. Even though she was no bigger than a minute and his hands were decently large, he worried about dropping her. All his muscles bunched as he set her down. He released the breath he'd been holding.

The straps weren't too difficult to manage.

He stepped aside when he was finished with them. "How'd I do?"

Melissa inspected his work, tugging at the straps to make sure they were solid.

"Pretty darn good for your first time, soldier." The corners of her lips turned up but the smile didn't reach her eyes.

Part of him wanted to make her laugh, to regain that easy feeling they'd once shared. There'd been glimmers of it since their reunion. But that was dangerous and his heart wouldn't survive another blow like the one she'd delivered last year. He couldn't afford to let his guard down no matter how nice it would be for the time being.

Colin held open her door for her before moving around to the driver's side and settling into his seat.

"She always this easy to take care of?" he asked.

"Pretty much. She's a good baby. We had a few bumps in the road early on but I'm pretty sure that was my inexperience," she said. "I'm thinking these little ones feed off the emotions around them more than we realize."

"I was just thinking that earlier." He started the engine. He put his hand on the gearshift and then paused. "I'm sorry about not being around during your pregnancy."

"That's not your fault," she said, sounding shocked.

He wanted to believe that was true. But that wasn't exactly the case, was it? If he'd acted more maturely she might've trusted him. He'd had no idea what she was going through. He'd been too busy licking his own wounds to realize that she might've been forced out of Bluff, out of her life by a ruthless criminal.

"Yeah, it was." He put the gearshift in reverse and backed out of his parking spot.

Melissa didn't respond. She didn't need to. Colin owned up to his mistakes.

The sky was layered with rolling gray clouds. On the ranch, Colin had learned to believe the weather. If there were thick dark clouds and the air was intense, that most likely did mean there was a bad storm on the way. Besides, his knees always let him know how much moisture there'd be in the air and they were creaking like he was 110 years old.

It took nearly a half hour to reach the nearest convenience store and they passed one car on the long, two-way road to the turn off for the lake. Storm or not, last night on the boat had been the perfect cover.

Every vehicle was suspect and traffic was picking up now that they were hitting one of the main roads in and out of the lake area. He was rethinking his idea to be in Oklahoma near Rancic's family home. It might be better to move on to Colorado and check out the place Rancic had been interested in. The one Melissa had told him about earlier. Having a place with no paperwork trail that could lead authorities back to Rancic was smart. There was a possibility that they'd find Rancic there. Give Colin five minutes alone with the guy and he didn't need a gun. He'd take him with his bare hands. But he had to consider his daughter first.

He parked near the air pump of the gas station and pulled out the throwaway cell phone. "I need to touch base with Dallas."

"Will you check on Tommy again?" she asked, and there was so much concern in her tone. She exited the truck long enough to get their daughter and return to her seat, cradling the baby.

"Yes." Colin didn't want to notice the compassion in her voice when she spoke about their friend. He didn't want to notice how great of a mother she seemed to be to their daughter. And she sure as hell didn't want to notice that she was even more beautiful than the year before. For someone who'd wanted to put off motherhood until a few years later, it sure looked good on her. It was impossible not to acknowledge how natural she was with Angelina. But then that little girl was an angel.

Melissa held their baby in her arms. Angelina's smiling face at such a contrast to the feelings going on inside him. What he had to say might tear Melissa's heart out.

"I was hoping that it wouldn't come to this," he started, "but I think we should take Dallas up on his offer to keep Angelina on the ranch. Before you say no, hear me out."

She nodded, her lips compressed together like she had to hold back her words.

"We need to go to Colorado and check out the place Rancic was looking at buying. What is it, by the way? Land? A hotel?"

"Both. The hotel is Mountain Trail Inn," she supplied.

"Okay. Say we check the place out. He might actually be there, which would put our daughter at risk. Besides, with the amount of care she needs, we'll be left vulnerable too often. If we're in a sticky situation and she cries at the wrong time, it's game over for all three of us. Rancic might not have put two and two together about me being her father but he might when he sees us together. At the very least he kills us and takes her, thinking that she belongs to him."

Melissa didn't answer right away and that was a good thing. It meant she was seriously considering his words.

"I'm not doubting my military skills but we have no idea how many men Richard could bring to a fight. My guess is that his brother is helping him at the very least," he said.

"The others in his organization probably won't," she said. "I'm pretty sure a few of them have been waiting for an opportunity like this. If Richard's out of the picture, they can handle Raymond a lot easier. But he's helped a lot of people and they might. Although, they tend to move through because they have problems of their own to deal with being on the run."

"I'm sure there's at least one more Rancic can trust and that's the best-case scenario. That would be three against one," he said. "Worst case, his entire network is looking for you."

She shot him a concerned look. "I can help."

"Fine, three against two, but you can't exactly handle a gun," he said. "And what little training I've been able to give you might not be enough. Not even with your instincts, which are strong."

She acknowledged his point with a nod.

"Those aren't bad odds if I'm full strength. With Angelina in the picture, it weakens both of our abilities to focus and we can't exactly stop to feed her in the middle of a gunfight. She cries, and she will cry, they'll be able to track us no matter where we go or how smart we think we are. She introduces too much of an unknown variable for me to have confidence I can keep you both safe. That has to be our top priority," he said. He was thinking solely on strategy and pushing his emotions aside. Even though he was professionally trained to do just that, the thought of leaving his little angel behind hit him square in the chest and harder than expected.

Melissa frowned and she hugged Angelina tightly. More proof that his words were making an impact.

"I thought the same thing last night on the boat," she said. "I was getting sick. You were trying to feed her and I figured if someone attacked us at that moment, there was no way we were coming out alive."

They sat in silence for a few more minutes. This wasn't the time to push for an answer. Colin would give her the space she needed to make a decision.

"I don't like the thought of being away from her," she finally said.

"Neither do I," he admitted.

"You've thought of every other possibility, haven't you?" she asked.

"Every scenario I can think of. Our best chance of staying under the radar was the boat. With the storms predicted to come through tonight, we have to stay on dry land. That will leave us exposed," he said.

"That's what I thought, too," she said.

Melissa hugged their daughter.

"Will Dallas be able to meet us somewhere for a handoff?" she asked.

Colin glanced in the rearview mirror. His gaze froze. "Change sides with me."

"What...*what* is it?" she asked, and it was

obvious that she'd picked up on the adrenaline rush coursing through him.

"I want you to take the wheel," he said with a forced calm.

Chapter Thirteen

Melissa glanced up in time to see a pair of men in a truck staring at them from twenty feet away.

"Dallas's license plate must've given us away," Colin said. "I don't think they know we've figured them out so no quick moves."

Melissa looked at the cooing baby in her arms and then at Colin. "What am I supposed to do with her while I drive?"

"Give her to me," he said, holding his arms out. "And then slowly slide over to take the wheel."

She handed over the baby, regretting that she hadn't given Angelina to Dallas sooner.

Melissa eased over to the driver's side as Colin fluidly slid over the seat. Angelina was lying against his chest, giggling. The motion must've tickled her tummy.

By the time Melissa buckled her seat belt, Angelina was strapped in.

"Get ready to go when I say," Colin said.

"Maybe I should walk over to them and shock them. Then you can take off with the baby," Melissa said, panic swelling in her chest.

"No way," Colin said. "I won't risk you."

"I guess there's no chance they haven't seen us," she said.

"None."

She watched in the rearview mirror as Colin—who was facing forward—slid the rear window open enough to fit a gun barrel through the opening.

"Where'd you get that?" she asked.

"From the glovebox last night." Colin dropped into position, ready to fire on the truck. "Ready?"

"Absolutely," she said. She'd made up her mind that nothing could happen to her daughter. Her resolve was the only thing keeping her from losing it. As adrenaline coursed through her, her hands began to shake.

"Drive away slowly," he said.

Melissa took a fortifying breath, put the gearshift in drive and stepped on the gas. She pressed a little harder than she'd intended and a few rocks spewed out from underneath her tires.

"Sorry," she said.

"You're doing great," Colin replied, his voice a study in calm. "Don't worry about checking behind you. I'll take care of them."

Colin's head had disappeared. She prepared herself for the *crack* sound that would come next.

Her nerves were strung so tight she thought they might snap. Her chest squeezed and breathing was difficult as she pulled onto the road.

"I was hoping for a cup of coffee before we had to party," Colin said with that calm and casual tone he was so good at during intense situations.

She couldn't help herself. She laughed.

"Good. I was hoping for that reaction," he said. "We're going to be fine. Believe that in your heart and it'll be true."

"Is that how you got through your missions in the military?" she asked.

"It is," he said.

"And it actually works?" she asked.

"Every time," he said.

She would absorb all the confidence that pulsed from him because her heart pounded wildly in her chest.

"What day is it today?" he asked.

"Monday, I think," she said, and she hated that her voice was as erratic as her pulse.

"What time is it?" he asked.

She glanced at the clock on the dashboard. "Seven forty-eight."

"Great," he said. "Take a left and then take the first on-ramp onto the highway."

It dawned on her why. "No stoplights?"

"That's right. We don't want to end up stuck at a light, plus it'll be easier for these guys to follow us in town," he said. "We have a better chance of disappearing in thick morning rush-hour traffic."

"Good point."

The men must've figured them out and realized they had a chance of escape because she heard a *crack*, the telltale sound of a handgun being fired.

Colin muttered the same curse she was thinking. Her heart stuttered. It was already pounding so hard it hurt.

Were they hit?

"Colin?" was all she could manage.

Another *crack* sound blasted in her ears.

Tires squealed behind them. She glanced in the rearview in time to see the truck swerving. She nailed the gas pedal and the truck got smaller and smaller until she saw it drive onto the embankment and stop.

Colin was beside her in the next heartbeat, checking her over.

"Is she—"

"The baby's fine," he said. "Pull off at the next exit."

"Are you hurt?" she asked as she did what he said. She hadn't dared look.

"We're okay," he said. "But we need to get out of here fast. Those guys back there most likely have friends. I blew out their front tire so we've slowed them down, but I have no idea how many we're up against and we have to assume the worst."

She had enough possession of her mental faculties to put on her emergency blinkers as she exited the highway and then pulled onto the side of the road. "That noise was so loud."

"I took care of her," he said. His tone was all business as he traded seats with her.

Melissa climbed over to check on their daughter as he buckled in. A second later, he sped away.

The baby's toothless grin tugged at Melissa's heart. The white headphones she had on were huge, covering most of the sides of her head.

"Dallas keeps those in the back for when he goes to the firing range," Colin said. "Her ears are fine."

Melissa buckled herself in with a sigh of relief. She took off the baby's headphones and Angelina cooed at her.

Colin cut the wheel a few times. Melissa couldn't be sure how many. She was too focused on her daughter and on being grateful that her little girl was safe.

But for how long?

COLIN HAD BEEN driving for more than two hours before he'd said it was safe enough to run through a fast-food chain's drive-thru. He'd already been in touch with Dallas to arrange to meet.

"I never thought a plain old cup of coffee could taste so good," Melissa said, enjoying every drop of that first sip.

"Every single cup tastes like heaven to me," he said with a wry smile.

The tension was starting to break from their earlier run-in with Richard's men. Colin had been too focused on making sure they were far away to get too comfortable. His grip on the wheel had been tight and his gaze intense on the stretches of highway in front of them. He'd made several defensive maneuvers, moved from highways to roads and back before exiting and then pulling under the golden arches.

Since then, the baby had been changed and fed, and slept peacefully. She was safe. *For now.* Those two little words wound through Melissa's mind.

They sat in the parking lot, waiting for Dallas to arrive, so she figured they might be somewhere in Texas. She hadn't kept up and decided the less she knew the better. She'd only stress more and she was trying to maintain a sense of calm with the baby around.

"After what happened, I'm convinced that we're doing the right thing by sending Angelina to the ranch with Dallas," she said after taking another sip. This was the meet-up point that Colin and Dallas had agreed on. She had no idea what town they were in and didn't care as long as they were far away from anyone connected to Richard.

"We are," he said.

"I'm shocked that she isn't traumatized by what happened this morning," Melissa said with a little more tension in her voice than she'd intended. It wasn't going to be easy to shake off the stress from the morning's events. Heck, when she added what they'd gone through last night, she figured she was doing pretty darn well under the circumstances. "I know I am."

Colin took another sip of coffee before he spoke, and that made her believe he had something serious on his mind. "I can break out on my own to find Rancic. You can go with the baby to the ranch. It might be better that way for everyone involved."

"I never thought I'd say this but she's safer without me," she said. "He wants revenge and he won't stop until he destroys me."

"He hasn't figured out that the baby doesn't belong to him," Colin said after a brief pause.

"How do you know?" she asked.

"Those men are trained to use weapons. They missed the entire truck using a 9mm handgun. Do you know what the odds of that are?" he asked.

She had to admit that she could fit what she knew about guns in a thimble. "They must be pretty slim if you're bringing it up right now."

"So that means Rancic thinks Angelina belongs to him and he doesn't want anything to happen to her. You'll be safer if you stick close to the baby," he said, and she couldn't read his emotions. Did he want her to go? Did he not want her to go? She had no idea.

Melissa could admit that the sexual current running between them had been a distraction neither could afford if they wanted to stay alive. This morning was a stark reminder of how serious this situation was. Even if the men hadn't intended to hit the truck, they could've. She knew enough about guns to realize that some were more accurate than others.

Richard had used a shotgun on Tommy, and stray fragments could've hurt her and the baby.

Granted, Tommy was in the opposite direction the whole time.

It suddenly occurred to her that the only reason she was still alive was most likely because she was standing in front of the car where Angelina was strapped in her car seat. If Richard had had a shot that couldn't possibly hit the baby, he would've taken it.

He must not've known whether or not he'd hit Tommy or he would've turned around.

So, all that really meant was that he really didn't want to get caught. He'd said that he'd never go back to jail.

The thought that the only thing keeping Melissa alive was her daughter struck hard.

"I'm sticking with you," she said. "Richard wants me dead, not Angelina. He'll deal with me first and then come after her later. Is there any chance he won't be able to figure out that she's still with me?"

"We can assume that he believes you have her or he wouldn't have ordered the men not to pull the trigger unless they had a clear shot," he said.

She'd overheard Colin asking Dallas to bring a baby doll earlier. Now, his request made sense.

A gray SUV pulled into the parking lot and then parked alongside them. Melissa had al-

ready noticed that Dallas was driving and
Gideon was in the passenger seat.

Her heart pounded as she thought about
being away from her daughter. They hadn't
been separated since Angelina was born.
Not to mention she was about to trust Dallas
O'Brien with the most important thing in her
life, her daughter. Somewhere down deep, and
no matter how hard her heart wanted to fight it,
she realized that it would be safer for Angelina
to go with him—to be away from her—until
law enforcement had a chance to find Richard
or they had a chance to stop him.

Dallas slid into the backseat and they ex-
changed somber greetings.

"She eats every four hours during the day
and five to six at night," Melissa said, immediately launching into how to care of her baby.

Dallas listened and nodded.

"She likes to have her back patted and get
some tummy time after a shower but you have
to be right next to her. A story at bedtime is her
favorite and I usually play classical music to
calm her down." It was her nerves doing that,
causing her to spew out everything she could
think to tell him about Angelina.

Neither O'Brien spoke. Both patiently listened.

"There's another option for you," Colin said

to her when she finished. "I can keep both of you alive if you hear me out. But you're going to have to trust that I know what I'm doing. Richard knows how devoted you are to your daughter, right?"

"Yes, he does," she said.

"And so he knows you well enough to realize that you wouldn't separate from her, right?" Colin asked.

"Of course." Her heart still argued against the idea of being away from her child, even for a few days.

"We've had an influx of kids at the ranch so one more won't raise any eyebrows. Besides, everything she needs is right there. No need to leave the property and you already know how tight security is. We won't have to add any personnel or do anything that would signal to Richard that anything's changed. He no doubt has people watching since you're his primary target, so they'll be extra careful."

Right again. Melissa nodded a third time.

"So, as soon as your location leaks he'll head directly toward you," Colin said.

"What if…" She couldn't even bring herself to say the words.

"I'll be there 24/7," Dallas offered. "She'll stay with me and Kate while you guys lead Richard far away and to his arrest."

"Unless you agree to go into protective custody right now," Colin said.

Had he been saving this so he could drop the bomb last minute? "I already told you how I feel about us being separated. It's bad enough that I won't be with our daughter, let alone be stuck in a strange city with no idea what was going on."

She realized her mistake almost the instant the slip left her mouth.

Dallas's gaze shot toward Colin, who gave a nod of acknowledgment. The brothers were so close that they didn't need words in a situation like this. Dallas now knew that Angelina was Colin's daughter. If it bothered him, he didn't show it. If he had questions—and who wouldn't?—he didn't ask.

"Think about what I said because we're reaching a point of no return here," Colin said.

Did he want her to go away from him?

She studied his expression and decided the answer was *no*.

The US Marshals service had failed her already. The O'Brien brothers were her best chance.

"I'm not going to the law," she said as panic nearly tore a hole in her chest, thinking about handing Angelina over. "If anything happens to me or Colin, though, she has no one else."

Melissa looked directly at Dallas. He was the eldest brother and could be the most intense. He was tall, like Colin, and similarly muscled. His hair was blacker and his eyes a little darker. He smiled less than Colin and already had the worry lines to prove it.

"She has all of us and we're her family, too," Dallas said and then promised, "but we won't let it come to that. Richard is going to jail and both of you are coming home."

"That's my plan," Colin said.

"I'll get her safely to the ranch. There's no question about that," Dallas added. "Once we're there, no one will touch her so I don't want you to worry." He paused a beat. "I know that's probably a tall order but I want you to know that we'll take good care of her."

"I wouldn't trust her with anyone else," Melissa said. She'd always loved the O'Briens and her daughter couldn't be in better hands.

"Your truck has been made," Colin said to Dallas. "I know I already told you that but it bears repeating."

"We're ditching it a couple of blocks from here. Gideon knows someone who'll keep it in their garage while they strip it," Dallas said, and his expression changed as he looked at Colin.

"What is it?" Colin asked.

"You need to know that a story broke in this morning's newspaper about Dad," Dallas said, and his voice was steady.

"I'm sorry that I haven't had a chance to warn you. I figured that might be coming," Colin said. "I'm guessing there were some pretty damning pictures involved."

Dallas nodded.

"Richard used those to pressure Melissa into going through with a wedding when she tried to change her mind," Colin said.

Dallas muttered a curse low and under his breath. "We should've known something else was going on."

"I'm sorry I didn't tell you before," she said, tearing up. "There was so much going on and I thought I could protect your family if I just did what he said."

"We know now," Colin said. "And that's what matters."

"Agreed," Dallas said. "Now the SOB needs to pay for what he's done."

"If you're ready, we should go," Colin said.

Melissa got out of the cab and took her daughter out of the car seat, reminding herself that this was the best way to keep Angelina safe.

"Gideon packed the trunk of the SUV with a few supplies he thought you'd be able to use in the coming days," Dallas said. "A few of us will join you as soon as we can."

Colin walked over to Gideon and then shook his hand.

"Take her now," she said to Dallas, handing her daughter to him. "Richard won't expect you to have her since he knows I'm not in Bluff."

Dallas took the sleeping little girl.

"And Dallas. Please keep her safe," she said, shoving down the ache in her chest at watching him preparing to walk away with Angelina.

"I understand what's at stake," Dallas said.

"Are you sure you want to do this?" she asked. "Richard is a dangerous man, and if he finds out you're involved with me in any way he'll try to destroy you and everything you love."

"I know the risk I'm taking," Dallas said. "My family doesn't shy away from doing the right thing because it's difficult."

She stood there, thinking how much a contrast Richard was to the O'Brien family.

"Thank you, Dallas," she said.

"It's time to get on the road," Colin said, moving next to her. His jaw was set. Determination darkened his eyes. And even though he tucked it down deep, she could see pain in his eyes.

Melissa knew that allowing Dallas to take Angelina away was the absolute right decision and yet her heart felt like it was being ripped out of her chest as she took the baby doll from Gideon. She couldn't allow herself to think that this was the last time she'd see her daughter. The thought nearly brought her to her knees.

No matter what else happened, Angelina was safe. Melissa repeated those words over and over again as Dallas turned and then walked away. With every step he took in the opposite direction, Melissa's heart ached a little bit more.

Before she had time to analyze her actions, she was reaching for Colin. His arms closed around her as the first tears fell. She buried her face in his chest, unable to watch the truck pull away and disappear as the sun kissed the western horizon.

"It'll only be for a couple of days," he said, and his voice was soft and warm against her neck where his face was nestled. She felt his heartbeat, steady and strong.

Melissa wrapped her arms around him, holding on like tomorrow was a question instead of a guarantee. Reality said that that was true. There were no more certainties while Richard was free. And the pain of being away from her daughter nearly impaled her. She tightened her grip around Colin.

"She's safe," he said, his lips moving against her skin. "He won't get to her. No one will ever hurt our daughter."

It wasn't the first time he'd spoken those last two words together. But this time was different. In them, there was hope for a future for the three of them. No matter what happened in the coming hours or days, Melissa would cling to that thought—the one where Angelina grew up with loving parents who were able to set aside differences and always put her first.

All they had to do was live long enough to see her again.

They stood there for a moment that stretched and extended around them. Cars and trucks zipped in and out of the parking lot; a busy place provided the best cover. None of the activity really registered. Her world shrank down to the two of them, together, in their own world as they looked into each other's eyes.

Melissa could pinpoint the exact second when her emotions turned from sadness and desperation to awareness—awareness of Colin's strong arms holding her upright, awareness of his muscled chest pressed against her breasts, awareness of him, male and virile and strong.

Colin repositioned his hands, cupping her face and tilting her head. He dipped down and pressed his lips to hers.

His eyes were closed, so she closed hers, too.

The taste of coffee was still on his lips.

Her body flush with his, she could feel his need—a need that matched hers. She wanted to be naked and tangled around him.

She wanted to feel his warm athletic body— all muscles and strength—molded to hers. She wanted to feel his weight on top of her, pressing her into the mattress.

She wanted to be happy again, if only for a short time.

And she wanted to get lost in that feeling.

Melissa couldn't be sure how long they stood there, kissing. Although, her body cried *not nearly long enough* when he pulled away.

He took in a sharp breath.

"We can't do this," he said in a low voice.

THE SUN DISAPPEARED across the highway by the time Colin took Melissa's hand and led her to the SUV. Melissa buckled up on the passenger side, ready for the long drive. The highway was flat for the rest of the drive through Oklahoma, Kansas and most of Colorado. It wasn't until they were close to Denver that the roads started winding up, down and around.

Not that it mattered. She couldn't quiet her mind enough to get any rest.

Melissa missed her little girl. All she could think about was Angelina making it to the ranch safely. She tried not to overthink everything that could go wrong with their plans. One bright spot so far was how well Tommy was recovering from surgery. And then there was kissing in the parking lot. For those moments in Colin's arms were the first in a year that Melissa felt like she was home.

The vehicle climbed and her ears started popping. By the time the SUV stopped, sleep was trying to take hold and she'd been dozing on and off for the last hour.

Colin moved the suitcase to the trunk after taking out and loading a handgun.

"I'll keep this under my seat, just in case," he said.

"Where are we?" she asked.

"At an old camp that I used to go to with the twins when we were young," he said, referring to his younger brothers Ryder and Joshua. "My uncle used to own and run the place. It closed years ago and nothing's been done with the land since. I know the area, which will keep us safer and it'll be easier to set a trap for Richard here. I wish you would've gone with Angelina, though."

"I know you do," she said. "You already made your position clear and so did I. He wants me dead. He'll come directly at me first. He would only use her if he couldn't get to me, which isn't going to be a problem. She's safer if she's not around me." Her voice broke on that last sentence. It was true. Colin knew it, too, or he never would've agreed to let her come along.

"Still, I don't like you being here," he said in a low growl. "I don't want him to get close to you."

"Then don't let him," she said. "But I'm sticking with you. We both know you're my best chance at staying alive."

Chapter Fourteen

The line between being there for the mother of Colin's child when she needed a shoulder to cry on or to feel safe in someone's arms and physically connecting with her was a fine thread. He'd be smart to remind himself to keep a safe distance, to keep in focus that Melissa was there so he could protect her for his daughter's sake. Losing her mother at such a young age would be a huge blow to the little girl.

That was totally being fair. Colin's feelings for Melissa ran deeper than wanting to keep her alive for their child's sake. He and Melissa had history. It was obvious they still had chemistry. There were too many times that he'd wanted nothing more than to take her into his arms and make love to her until she lay there exhausted like they'd done so many times in the past.

But that part of their relationship was in the past. Trying to recapture even a small slice of what they had would confuse an already complicated situation. Besides, a lot could change in a year. A lot *had* changed in a year, the annoying little voice inside his head reminded. And a whole lot more could change in the next twenty-four hours.

He needed to stay focused or they'd both end up dead. There was no way he'd allow Angelina to grow up an orphan. Thoughts of those big eyes, round cheeks and her smile breathed new resolve into him.

"We'll bunk down for a few hours in the car for the rest of the night," he said, locating a blanket in the backseat. He placed it over her. "Lay your chair back and try to get in as much sleep as you can. I need you as well rested as possible come morning."

COLIN HAD BARELY closed his eyes when the first light peeked through the windshield. He'd scarcely moved when Melissa bolted upright, practically gasping for air.

"You're okay," he said, keeping his voice level so he didn't give away his true level of concern.

"He was here," she said, out of breath. Her gaze darted around.

"It's just me." Between her flinching every time he reached for her unexpectedly and the nightmare, he was beginning to see the true scars from the past year. Richard had to be stopped. Colin was starting to get a better picture of what her life must've been like.

Melissa relaxed on an exhale when she seemed certain that she was safe. She fumbled around for the lever on her right and then repositioned her seat in the upright position.

Colin grabbed the pack from the backseat and pulled out bottled waters, toothpaste and toothbrushes. Seeing Melissa's panic first thing didn't do good things to his blood pressure and made him want to punish Rancic even more. Colin also realized that Melissa had been living in a prison.

He held out her toothbrush. She took the offering without saying anything. Mostly, she just looked shaken and Colin fought the urge to take her in his arms.

They exited the car and moved near a towering pine. It was still chilly this time of year in the mountains. Beautiful, but cold. Colin missed Texas, warm sunshine and the ranch even more as he brushed his teeth.

A random thought struck. Could he convince Melissa to live on the ranch? She would need her own place but there was plenty of land and spots to build. They could figure out a way to make it work. He'd offer his house to Melissa and Angelina while having something more suitable built.

After rinsing toothpaste out of his mouth using bottled water, he surveyed the area. He'd memorized the camp layout and these woods years ago but everything looked different now, smaller. He probably should've expected that.

Melissa was a quiet shadow as he walked the perimeter of the cabins. There were a dozen, half on one side of the main gathering area, half on the other, just like he remembered from spending time here with the twins. A couple of chaperones kept boys and girls separate. There wasn't much else needed at that age. Young boys mostly wanted to tease girls, tease and torture by pulling hair or toilet-papering cabins. The true spark wouldn't ignite for a couple more years. The cabins were set back and on either side of the mess hall.

A party room was to the left of the campfire, and an outdoor pavilion sat to the right. Behind the outdoor pavilion was a small shop to buy sweets and souvenirs.

The campfire was a circle in the middle and the center of activity. Logs still circled the rocked-off area where they'd lit the flame and had heard stories of the Old West.

Two feet of weeds covered much of the area now, choking out grass and flowers.

The air at this elevation was dry, so Colin would have to be careful when he lit a flame. He moved to the fire pit and then pulled weeds. Melissa worked silently beside him, following his lead.

Colin lit a fire and took out camping supplies. He made coffee using an iron pot. The air was filled with purpose. There was a lot to do between now and tonight.

"When will your brothers be here?" Melissa finally asked. "Did they text to let you know?"

"Yes. Before the sun goes down," he said, handing her a tin cup filled with fresh coffee. "I don't have any sweeteners."

"I don't need any today," she said, taking the offering. She took a sip. "This is amazing."

"There's a PowerBar in the backpack if you're hungry," he said, motioning toward the green bag.

"Maybe later," she said. "I'm not awake enough to eat yet."

Colin suspected there was more to it than that. She still seemed shaken by her nightmare. He didn't press. She'd talk when she was ready. He sat back on his heels and drank the dark liquid. It wasn't too bad.

"Where are we sleeping tonight?" she asked.

"You and me will be in the souvenir shop," he said.

She stared at one of the buildings. Something was on her mind. He could tell by the way she chewed on the inside of her jaw.

"Can I ask you a question?" she finally asked, settling next to him.

He nodded, stretching out his legs.

"Before, when I told you about what Richard said about your father. You didn't hesitate to defend him and neither did Dallas earlier. I know you both love him, but you especially are not the kind of person to let that love blind you. So, how do you know he didn't have an affair?" she asked.

"I can't be absolutely certain about anything. I know one thing. Two people never loved each other more than my parents," he said.

"How do you know that?" she asked.

He looked straight at her, into those brown eyes with violet streaks, and took in a sharp breath. "Because that's the way I loved you."

A few tears streamed down her cheeks and he thumbed them away. "Don't do that. Don't cry."

"The only way I could get through the day that I married Richard was by picturing you standing there, not him," she said. "He turned my stomach but I had to help my father. I was so confused and I couldn't stand by and watch my father go to jail. He was wrong. He did things that were bad and part of me wants to condemn him for it. But the other part, the side that won, remembers how he used to sing those old bluegrass songs to put me to sleep after Mom died."

She stopped long enough to release a few sobs.

Colin put his arm around her waist and, in one motion, swept her beside him. Their outer thighs touched and he felt the same trill she did based on her reaction to the contact.

"He was all I had growing up and he did the best he could," she said, and her voice held less sorrow now. "Without him, I was afraid of being all alone."

"You had me, my family," he said in a low voice. He understood not being able to turn her back on her father. Colin was even more grateful for his own parents in comparison.

"I know. But how could I turn to you?" she asked.

"We were building a life together, Melissa," he said. "You don't think I would've understood about your father? Helped him?"

"Please don't be upset. I was embarrassed. I was marrying *you*. Your family is perfect. They have principles and do the right thing for other people even if it means they could get hurt. *You're* perfect. I'm not," she said. "Besides, I had no way out. This was about more than money. Richard had proof that my dad had doctored the books on the business he'd planned to buy from him."

"You should've trusted me enough to be honest about what was going on," Colin said.

"And then what? You're impulsive, Colin, and used to getting your way in life. Would you have honestly been able to step aside?" she asked.

He started to argue but she stopped him.

"You could never let an injustice like that stand without trying to do something to stop it," she countered.

Colin thought hard about what she was saying. The truth wasn't always the easiest thing to hear.

He picked her up and sat her on his lap, facing him. At this vantage point, they could see eye to eye, which was good because she needed to see the sincerity in his. "My family is far from perfect. See that tree over there? The one with the big branch? I let my brother fall off it because I thought he needed to learn a lesson."

"Doesn't exactly make you a criminal," she said.

"Except that he broke his arm in two places

and I really did it because I was mad at him. Summer camp was over after that, like I knew it would be if something happened, and I didn't want to be here to watch my brothers anyway when I could be home, hanging out with my friends," he said.

"You were a kid," she said.

"I was fourteen. Old enough to know better," he said. "My girlfriend had broken up with me because she didn't want to be alone during the summer. I blamed my brothers so I rebelled and didn't take care of them like I should've."

"That's not the same as pushing him off the limb," she said, staring into his eyes. The air had changed and they both seemed aware of the position they were in.

"True. But I could've stopped him. I saw the danger. First week of camp a kid fell off that exact same spot and had to be sent home," he said. "All I could think about was getting back to Bluff so I could win Leslie back."

Melissa didn't speak for a long moment. She just looked into his eyes. It was the most honest moment he'd had in a long time. Being with her, spending time with her, cracked the casing he'd built around his heart. He didn't want to allow light inside the dark places. He didn't want to need anyone again the same way he needed her. That annoying little voice inside his head said it was too late. He'd reopened that wound and when this was over, he was going to feel worse than the last time if that was even possible.

"Melissa." He gripped her waist tighter.

"Colin." Those intelligent eyes of hers stared beyond the physical.

"Why did you really leave?" he asked. "Was it me?"

"You? It was never your fault, Colin. I'm all my father has and it's just been us. I never stopped loving you but I'm not good enough for you. Know that whatever happens in the next couple of days that my heart always belonged to you," she said. And then she kissed him.

Chapter Fifteen

"I wish you would've trusted me," Colin said wrapping his arms around Melissa tighter, pulling her body flush with his as she molded around him, still in his lap. Heat zinged through her as the current built inside her.

His hands roamed her body, erasing the past, the torment, making her feel alive and like a real woman again. In that moment, Melissa finally felt that the world had righted itself even though it wouldn't last. She tunneled her hands through his dark hair.

Shifting position, she ground her sex against his full erection. Her body cried out to touch him, to feel him moving inside her one more time.

Colin drove his tongue into her mouth. He tasted like coffee and peppermint toothpaste, two of her favorite flavors mixed together. She sucked on the tip of his tongue and his grip tightened around her hips.

He brought his hands around to the front and cupped her full breasts in his palms. Her nipples beaded and so much hunger welled up from deep inside that her hands shook.

She kissed him harder.

The next thing she knew, her shirt was being pulled up. She grabbed the hem and helped shrug out of it, aiding its removal. She tugged at his next and they managed to have it off and piled with hers a couple of seconds later. Her bra was a quick third.

"You're beautiful," Colin said, stopping long enough to take in her partially naked form.

She should be embarrassed by the fact that she was half-naked and in the middle of a campground. There was something about being with Colin that made everything seem natural, right, like life was just the way it was supposed to be, if only temporarily.

A breeze blew across her sensitized skin as her hands moved straight to Colin's zipper. He managed to remove his jeans and boxers without upsetting her position as she straddled him. The rest of her clothing followed suit just as seamlessly, as if this was a dance they'd rehearsed a hundred times. Maybe they had. Making love had always been a beyond-this-world experience with Colin. His easy charm, intelligence and dark good looks were so good at seducing her.

Melissa was tired of fighting her feelings for him, her attraction—an attraction that had her feeling so natural with him, naked and outside.

His erection pulsed against her and need engulfed her. She guided his tip inside her and he released a guttural groan. His fingers tightened around her hips, easing her down on top of him. His entire body was chorded as she took him in. And then his hands were on her breasts.

"You're perfect," he managed to say before their mouths fused together.

She bucked her hips and his hands fell back to her waist, driving her up and down until the pressure built and the emotions skyrocketed and tension reached a peak. She rocked faster and he thrust harder until both were on the edge, begging for release, their bodies in perfect motion. She tipped over first and then he followed.

"I still love you," Colin said quietly, his lips moving against her neck. "I can't lose you again."

"I love you, Colin." And those words changed everything.

COLIN'S BROTHERS WOULD arrive soon and there was a lot to do in order to be ready. He'd spent the balance of the day mapping the area around the cabins as though their lives depended on it. They did. He'd retraced his steps several times, memorizing every tree, every possible escape route, and every potential hazard.

There was a pond on the far east side of the site. A creek cut across the property in a near-straight line, running north to south. Just below camp, it pooled into a sizable swimming hole. Colin remembered the bright orange vests counselors had strapped on them before allowing them time in the water.

A set of teepees clustered on the west side of camp. The camp was straightforward, a throwback to simpler days. Or maybe it just seemed simple when all Colin had had to think about was keeping the twins out of trouble. The older he got, the more he was beginning to realize that life got a lot more complicated with age. He needed to change with the times, too. Maybe it was time to outgrow his black-and-white approach toward life and start acknowledging that it wasn't that simple. His feelings for Melissa would certainly fall in the gray area. In the past, he'd have looked at her actions as a flat betrayal, and he had done just that for the past year. There would be no coming back from that.

After what he'd learned, Melissa's situation couldn't have been more complex. She loved her father, and Richard had used that love against her to manipulate her. The man had also used her love for Colin and his family. He clenched his back teeth thinking about it.

To complicate matters, there was a child involved.

And then there were Colin's feelings for Melissa. He could acknowledge that he'd never stopped loving her. He could further acknowledge that her leaving him fell under the category of extenuating circumstances. The hardest part for him to swallow now was that she hadn't believed in him enough to tell him what was really going on. What kind of a life could they build together without trust?

Colin could go round and round on that question until his head spun. He glanced at his watch. His brothers should be arriving sometime within the next two hours.

"What's next?" Melissa asked. She hadn't strayed more than two feet from him since making love this morning. Not that he could say that he minded. He liked having her near, and it was more than just so he could watch over her. He wasn't ready to analyze what that meant.

"We clean out a cabin as a decoy. One of my brothers will be in a different one, close enough to watch," he said, walking into the first cabin. He wedged the door open to allow sunlight inside. Melissa stopped at the door.

"I'm not going in there," she said. Something moved in a dark corner. It was probably a field mouse but Melissa jumped anyway. "There have to be about a thousand spiders."

"Okay, this one's out." He linked their fingers and led her to the next one with a wry grin. "I'm guessing going inside one of these to make love again is out of the question."

She tugged at his hand to make him stop.

"We can make love again, just not in one of those," she said.

He didn't waste time hauling her into his arms. She pushed back.

"Hold on," she said. "Is that swimming hole safe?"

"Should be," he said.

He'd barely answered when she took off down the hill, stripping off clothes as she ran. The sun was out and it was warmer now.

Colin followed suit, both of their garments littering the trail behind them.

The water was cold but her skin was warm against his. He picked her up, she wrapped her legs around his midsection and he drove himself inside her, home.

With their bodies pressed together and her

arms tangled around his neck, Colin shut out the questions in his mind and made love to her. This time, they moved slow and sweet, savoring every kiss and the feel of being completely connected. He'd missed this…the feeling of being one with Melissa…of being lost with her.

"That was amazing," she finally said, breathless from making love.

"Once this is over we have some decisions to make," he said, not quite ready to examine the implications of what was happening between them.

"Yeah," she said, "like how are we going to dry off and not freeze to death first?"

He squeezed her sweet round bottom and pressed his erection against her belly. "Who said we were done?"

WHETHER HE LIKED it or not, Colin had a shadow. Based on the way he stopped every once in a while to pull her into an embrace or plant a sweet kiss on her lips, Melissa didn't think he minded.

Her heart wanted to believe that what was happening between them was real again, that it was something they could build on.

"You should probably try to get some rest before my brothers arrive," he said. "There's no telling when Richard will show now that my brothers have put out word."

"What about law enforcement?" she asked.

"We'll get all that information when my brothers arrive, which should be soon," he said.

"It makes me nervous that we haven't been able to make contact with them," she said.

"They won't come if it's not safe," Colin said, setting up a sleeping bag and a rifle in the woods near the campsite. He'd located a spot below the campfire and above the spillway they'd made love in. "I'd feel better if you weren't here when this all goes down."

"Where else would I go?" she asked, her nerves set on edge.

"I'm not letting you out of my sight. You're safest with me," he said, glancing up from the scope he'd trained on the door of the decoy cabin. "I just wish I could tuck you somewhere safe."

"I just hope he falls for it," she said. "This is a lot to coordinate."

"That's true," he admitted, and she was glad that he wasn't sugar-coating the situation. "I know you're scared. We'll let law enforcement do their jobs as soon as we have Richard on-site and we make the call. Until they get here, I'll do what I have to in order to protect you. Two of my brothers will be awake, one inside that cabin." He pointed to the one directly across from the decoy. "The other will be in the mess hall. Both will be armed and ready to go. One will make the call to law enforcement as soon as Richard shows. All we have to do is trap and detain the man. They'll do the rest."

"A lot can go wrong and we don't know if he'll show or send someone else." She sat down on the sleeping bag. She hoped it would be as easy as it sounded.

"If he thinks you're here with a few of us and no law, he'll bite," he said, sitting up. He pressed a kiss to her temple. "Believe it or not, I've done missions like this before."

"But what if things don't go as planned?" she asked.

"I've thought through all the possibilities, even the ones that include me not making it out alive, and believe me, Richard won't go free," he said with so much sincerity, so much confidence, that she almost believed it, too.

She couldn't even think about anything happening to Colin.

He must've picked up on the tension cording inside her when he said that last part because he said, "Nothing's going to happen to me. I just have to consider all the worst-case scenarios."

"And if something happens to me instead?" she asked. "What about that?"

"There isn't a case in which I will allow that to happen. Period. Angelina needs her mother, and my family is committed to making sure she has you." His voice was steady and steel and reassuring even though she probably shouldn't let it be. There was so much determination that she couldn't help herself.

"She needs her dad, too," Melissa said, placing a kiss on Colin's lips. "And I need you. I tried to live my life without you, Colin. It didn't work. None of this works without you."

Surprisingly, a few tears sprang from her eyes.

He kissed one as it rolled down her cheek.

"Then I better be damn careful because I have no intention of letting you down."

Chapter Sixteen

"Stay low," Colin said to Melissa as he saw an occasional flash of light as a vehicle twisted and turned along the road leading to the camp. He'd already heard the Jeep's engine as it wound up the road. The horn honked twice. Then, nothing for two beats before a third beep sounded.

"They're here." Colin popped to his feet before offering a hand up to Melissa. She accepted the help and then he held on to one of her hands as they walked to the Jeep.

Colin let go long enough to embrace his brothers, Joshua and Austin. "Where's Tyler?"

Joshua must've seen the panic in Melissa's eyes because he said, "Angelina is doing great and she's safe on the ranch."

"Thank you," Melissa said.

"As for Tyler, he's hanging around at the camp entrance. Ryder stayed back to care for his pregnant wife and offer reinforcements at the ranch." Joshua held up his cell phone. "We'll be in constant contact."

"You guys already know Melissa," Colin said.

Austin leaned in for a hug even though his gaze trained on Colin and Melissa's linked fingers. "Good to see you again."

He'd give them an update as soon as he figured out what the hell was going on between them.

Joshua echoed Austin's sentiment, also reaching in for a quick hug. He seemed less interested in the two holding hands. His law enforcement training would keep him focused on the situation at hand and Colin was grateful. "Angelina is a little sweetheart. You guys did good, and I want you both to know that she's being well cared for."

"I've never seen Janis, the housekeeper, happier now that we have so many kids on the ranch," Austin said. He smiled, even though Colin knew his brother's situation had been gnawing at him. His wife, Maria, had left him and their relationship status was up in the air. Austin wasn't talking about it. The subject was off-limits, which didn't signal good things. No one pressed for information. His brother knew that any one of them would be there for him in a heartbeat when he was ready to open up about it.

"You being here means a lot," Colin said to Austin, acknowledging his sacrifice.

"I just wish Mom and Dad could've met their grandkids," Austin said, redirecting the conversation. He was good at avoiding talking about what was really on his mind.

"I was crushed to hear about your parents," Melissa said. "I had no idea anything had happened or I would've come."

"We appreciate the thought," Joshua said.

"Any closer to figuring out who was behind it?" she asked.

Colin had been so wrapped up in keeping her and the baby safe that he hadn't had time to check in with his brothers on the case.

"The investigation has been set back with Tommy in the hospital. His deputies are volunteering for shifts to look through Hollister McCabe's papers. He'd forced the Hattie family out of town for their land," Joshua said.

"Their ranch backs up to yours, doesn't it?" she asked. She didn't seem fazed by the fact that Hollister McCabe would be involved in something illegal. It would be no surprise to anyone who knew him, and his reputation extended far beyond Bluff.

"It does," Joshua said. "Tommy was on to

something before he was shot. He'd called Dallas and said that he wanted to meet with us. I'd imagine all that's going to be on hold while he heals. His recovery is everyone's top priority."

Austin seemed to anticipate the next question. He held his hand up. "He's doing much better. Doc McConnell brought in a special surgeon to make sure they got all the bullet fragments out of his ribs. He has a long way to go to heal but he's talking and asking for food."

"That's a good sign," Colin said.

Melissa smiled. It didn't reach her eyes. He could see the worry in the lines of her forehead. "I wondered…I'm afraid… There's a possibility that *he* could be behind what happened to your parents." Guilt washed over her. She stared at a spot on the ground. "Early on, he was convinced that I was still in love with Colin and he was right. He might've done that to get to me. I didn't even know what had happened."

Tears free-fell.

"It's not your fault," Colin said, and both of his brothers were quick to agree.

"What if it is and they're dead because of me, because I wasn't convincing enough?" She just stood there, looking so bereft.

"He targeted you. He manipulated you. But he didn't break you," Colin said. "Remember that."

"If Richard killed our parents, that's on him, not you," Joshua said emphatically. "And we'll make sure justice is served for everything he's done to this family. Because when he took you away from us, he didn't just take a shot at my brother, he hurt all of us."

"I'm so sorry." Melissa threw her arms around Colin's neck.

"You did nothing wrong," Colin said, and he meant it. Anger welled inside him. He shot a look at Joshua, who nodded in response.

Rancic would be added to the suspect list once they returned to Bluff.

And if it turned out that man was responsible, there'd be more than hell to pay for his actions.

"I REMEMBER THIS PLACE," Joshua said to Colin as he studied the area from the center point, the fire pit.

"We were kids the last time we were here," Colin said. "Not too much has changed."

Colin hadn't been sure what kind of reaction Melissa would get from his brothers and was grateful they'd welcomed her with open arms. He had a lot of catching up to do with them. Hell, first he needed to figure out his and Melissa's relationship for himself. All he knew was that he wanted her in his life. The details of what that meant would have to come later.

"That's a good thing," Joshua said. "We don't have much sun left. I'll want to walk the perimeter before it gets dark."

"Someone followed us most of the way here. We let him believe we didn't know," Austin said. "Lost him as we got close by cutting through Denver."

Joshua had worked for Denver PD before returning to the ranch to take his rightful place. He would know the area well enough to easily lose someone and, more importantly, had the law enforcement contacts they would need to pull off an arrest.

"There were two in the car and they'll alert Richard. After talking it over with Joshua and doing some calculations, our best guess is that Richard will most likely be in the area sometime tonight. He'll have to drive if he wants to get anywhere near us and if he isn't stopped on the way here, which is a possibility, it'll take him a minute to figure out where we are. Took us nearly two hours to make it up the mountain," Austin added.

"Have you discussed the right time to bring in law enforcement?" Colin asked. He wasn't planning on taking any chances when it came to Melissa. If he could avoid a confrontation with Richard, that would be the best-case scenario. Although, there was a very big part of him that just wanted ten minutes alone with Rancic.

"Joshua's planning to make the call to law enforcement about a sighting at first light," Austin said. "He'll call his old supervising officer."

Melissa stiffened next to him.

"So, Richard is here by morning, possibly earlier," he recapped, taking her hand in his.

"But that means Richard could be here and gone before they set foot on camp soil," Melissa finally spoke, and her voice was shaky.

"We've accounted for that possibility," Austin said. "That's a risk we're going to have to take. We doubt there's been a leak in law enforcement but we can't ignore the chance, either. We just don't know at this point, and we can't risk Richard knowing that law enforcement will be involved until the last minute. It's the best way to protect you."

"What's your professional opinion about law enforcement being involved?" Colin asked Joshua.

"It's unlikely but not impossible." Joshua rubbed the scruff on his chin. "There's a better chance Rancic managed to pick up on communications by stealing Marshal Davis's laptop and phone."

"Which means it's safe to assume that when we reach out to law enforcement, he'll know," Colin said.

"I believe so," Joshua said. "We'll need to get moving. We don't have a lot of time to familiarize ourselves with the plan or practice."

Colin knew the implications of that from his military training. There was a reason so many former servicemen and women made careers in law enforcement when they were discharged. Colin was proud to serve his country and there was no other option in his mind for him to return to the ranch afterward. The only thing he loved as much as his country was the land he lived on and worked.

Joshua walked the perimeter as Colin caught Austin up-to-date.

"Did it all come back to you?" Colin asked Joshua when he returned.

"Amazing how little has changed," he said. "Saw that you're set up with a rifle in the tree line between the outdoor pavilion and the swimming hole beneath. That's smart. With the way the road winds up, you'll have a great vantage point."

"True. My gut says he's not coming at us straight, though," Colin said. "I can still see the entrance and reposition as needed. But my money is on the fact that he'll come in from behind the mess hall or one of the sides, which would be the cabins."

"Agreed," Joshua said as the last of the sunlight disappeared.

"I set up camp for you guys in one corner of the mess hall. It's too easy a guess for you to be set up in one of the girls' cabins and Rancic doesn't strike me as stupid. He's a criminal, but not incompetent, and it would be dangerous to underestimate him."

"True," Joshua said as Austin nodded.

"I cleaned up one of the cabins anyway and made it seem like I didn't want him to check one on the boys' side by leaving tracks leading up to the door. Just enough to make it seem like there might actually be someone inside," Colin said.

"From the mess hall I can watch both," Joshua said.

"It's the biggest barrier for us visually and the easiest way for him to come in from the backside without being noticed. He'll most likely come that way and then splinter off before he gets to the building," Joshua said.

"That's what I would do," Colin agreed.

"The main variable is how many men he

has working for him or will bring with him," Joshua said.

Austin nodded. "He has a brother who's gone missing. We can assume those two are working together." He turned to Melissa. "How many others does he associate with on a regular basis?"

"Half a dozen," she supplied.

Colin could almost feel the thin sheen of ice coating her words when she spoke about Richard. Thinking of what she'd endured, of the life his child had been brought into even for a few months, caused heat to pour off him in waves.

"We came in contact with a pair yesterday morning," Colin said. "So we know of at least two more on the job."

"Or they could be included in the six you said Melissa mentioned to you. No way to know for sure. Either way, we'll prepare for a small army," Joshua said.

Melissa gasped.

Colin wanted to reassure her, tell her everything would be okay. Right now, their future was uncertain. And the situation was as unpredictable as a spring thunderstorm.

All he could do was wrap his arm around her waist and hold her.

MELISSA COULDN'T SLEEP. It came as no surprise. As the sun went down, the cold settled in again.

She thought about the irony of spring, the clash of cold leftover from winter with the warmth from the promise of summer. She thought about how their interaction caused powerful storms—storms big enough to produce tornadoes that could devastate an entire town. Richard was cold—he'd tried to keep her in his icy grip. And Colin was the opposite.

The thought of those two systems crashing into each other, the fallout that would follow, took her breath away. The more Melissa had listened to plans to take down Richard, the more tension had tightened her shoulder blades. Her life with Richard had been like living in an arctic cave. Colin was the sun—the promise of warmth and sunshine and better days.

Both of those lives were about to clash.

The O'Briens had brought plenty of ammunition to the fight. So would Richard. She said a silent prayer that there'd be no bloodshed by morning, even though everything inside her said there would be.

She sucked in a deep breath.

"What is it?" Colin asked. They'd set up in the small gift shop behind the outdoor pavilion for a few hours of sleep. His warm body was flush with hers. Her head was on his chest, and she'd settled into the crook of his arm.

"Thinking about tomorrow," she said. Austin had joined Tyler in the mess hall for a few hours of sleep while Joshua took a shift keeping watch at the front entrance. "About trying to figure out a way we all get out of this alive. If anyone gets hurt…"

"It won't be your fault. Rancic didn't just target you. He targeted our family." Colin pressed a kiss to her forehead. "If you want to change your mind about being here, we can disappear. Take Angelina and get out of the country if you want. I've been thinking a lot about it. We only have to stay away long enough for law enforcement to catch Richard."

"And always be looking over my shoulder? Never knowing when he might show up or hurt our daughter?" she said. "We need to end this now while Angelina's safe at the ranch."

"I'd feel better about this whole scenario if you were tucked away somewhere safe, too," he said, and there was so much honesty in his voice.

"There's no one who can protect me better than you," she said, and she meant it. No one would love her more or care more about her going home to take care of Angelina than Colin. His brothers came in a close second. "The ranch is the perfect place for her to be, and there's nowhere I'd rather be than here with you. We're going to take that monster down and not live in fear of shadows anymore." Her resolve grew with every word. No matter what else happened tomorrow, Angelina would be safe.

Colin's grip tightened around her. "I love you, Melissa. When this is all over, we need to sit down and figure out how that changes things. Right now, all I want is to have you right where you are."

Melissa tilted her head up and kissed him. He wasn't making any promises to her, and she wasn't sure if that was because he had no idea what to do with their relationship or he wasn't the kind of man who would promise something that he wasn't certain he could deliver. The latter goose bumped her arms. "Promise me you won't do anything crazy when you see him."

And by *crazy* she meant do anything that might get himself killed.

"I promise to keep you safe above all else," he said.

She was afraid of that.

But for now, tonight, she wanted to make love to him in these last few hours while he belonged to her.

And that's exactly what she did.

Chapter Seventeen

Colin had an hour of shut-eye before he forced himself to wake. He'd battled back and forth on leading Richard away from Melissa for a fight before he'd let himself nod off.

Now that he was awake and his mind was clear, he wanted to stay right where he was a few more minutes, holding her. There'd been too many nights in the past year that he'd wished for this very thing, to have her back with him where she belonged.

His mind churned through scenarios one more time. There was an obvious problem with trying to lead Rancic away from camp. If Rancic figured out what Colin was doing, all he had to do was circle back. With Colin away, his brothers would be down a man.

No one had a clue how many men Rancic would bring to the fight.

But if there was any chance that Colin could

go at Rancic one-on-one, he wouldn't hesitate. One man against one man. A fair fight. But again, he had no idea how many people Richard planned to bring. Besides, the words *Rancic* and *fair fight* didn't even belong in the same sentence.

The possibility that Rancic would come alone was next to nil, so it wasn't worth spending too much time considering. There was a slight possibility that he wouldn't come at all. He could send someone in his place.

But Rancic wanted revenge. He wanted Melissa. And he wanted her to pay.

He was on the run and this was the first real chance he'd had at finding her. He had to know that the longer he was in the US, the more risk he was taking. Based on his volatile temperament, Colin figured the man would take the bait. He'd come fast, figuring that he could get to them before they had time to fortify the area.

He was almost right.

They had a few tricks up their sleeves, which was why Colin needed to stick with the plan. Any other scenario carried unnecessary risk— risk he couldn't afford to take with his brothers or the woman he loved. Yeah, he loved her. He loved Melissa. He'd never stopped.

So, rather than risk leaving her vulnerable

he would go along with the plan he and his brothers had developed last night. He would stay the course. The plan they'd come up with was the best they had to work with under the circumstances. Austin had set up in an adjacent cabin with his attention directed toward the decoy boy cabin. He was visible enough that Rancic might just believe he was there to protect Melissa. Colin's job was to set up at the rifle/sleeping bag location, and Tyler was situated under the outdoor pavilion. Again, his attention was set to the cabin.

Inside, they'd stuffed blankets on a lower bunk in the corner of the room to make it look like the shape of a woman. In reality, the only woman on the campus was in the souvenir shop tucked behind the counter sleeping. If she could wake and this whole ordeal be over without a scratch on anyone he loved, Colin wouldn't complain.

Enough time had most likely passed for Rancic to have figured out where they were after being tipped off. According to their calculations, 3:00 a.m. was the absolute earliest he could make it to the camp.

Colin untangled his body from Melissa's, missing her warmth the second he peeled out of the sleeping bag they'd shared. He zipped it up, tucking the corners around her to keep her warm. At this elevation, it was cold this time of year at night.

His watch read two thirty in the morning. He'd gotten just enough sleep to energize himself. He fired off a few push-ups to get his blood pumping and then threw on his hunter green hoodie. He'd blend in better at night with the dark color. If there was still snow on the ground, it would be a different story. Snow was up the mountain at higher elevations and so he was safe.

He moved around the counter in order to block Melissa from the light on his phone. She needed sleep and, if he had his way, she'd sleep right through everything that was about to go down.

Colin texted Joshua to let him know he was awake and moving toward his post. Joshua's shift at the entrance should finish soon and he would take his place in the mess hall. Colin had volunteered but everyone had agreed that it would be best for him to stick close to Melissa for as long as possible. Besides, Rancic would assume that Melissa was with Colin. That knowledge was his secret weapon because he had every intention of leading the man away from her. Leaving the souvenir shop would be difficult, but he needed to take his post.

The souvenir shop was protected from three

sides. The likelihood that Rancic would pay it much attention was miniscule. As a precaution, he'd left Melissa a P2K, a lightweight semiautomatic pistol, ready to shoot if necessary. Even though she'd grown up in Texas, she didn't have a lot of experience with guns. She'd been around plenty but that was different than needing to use one and especially once adrenaline kicked in.

Colin may have only met his daughter forty-eight hours ago, but he missed her from a place so deep he hadn't known it existed before. How something so tiny could take up so much space in a man's heart was something that he would never figure out. Angelina had.

Colin settled on top of the sleeping bag, staying low in order to stave off the cold night air. The wind bit through his jacket and the temperature had dropped a good twenty degrees, hovering near freezing.

He could cover pretty much everything and everyone from his vantage point. The outdoor pavilion was slightly to his right and in front of him. The souvenir shop was behind that. Tyler had a clear view from his vantage point, as well. With Austin in the cabin to the right of the decoy, they had solid coverage.

The girls' cabins were on the other side of the fire pit. If it were Colin, he'd check those first. No way would he go to the boys' side where everyone was stationed. He'd give the girls' side a fifty-fifty chance of being empty. Even so, he'd investigate there first after surveying the entire area and seeing that they wanted him to check out the first cabin on the boys' side.

Colin hoped everything would go according to plan. He almost laughed out loud. What mission had ever been executed flawlessly? He couldn't remember a single one. And that's why he'd stay alert and minimize distractions. Focus and patience won battles. Take the battle, win the war.

Cold settled on top of him like a blanket. He had to periodically flex and release his fingers to keep them from going completely numb.

More than two hours had gone by when he saw movement near the mess hall. *Yep.* Just like he'd figured. Through his rifle's scope, he picked up two figures.

Colin looked left, reaching for his phone to send out the warning signal. Out of the corner of his eye, he caught the outline of a dark male figure launching toward him. He must've followed the creek.

Instead of bracing himself against the force coming at him, Colin grabbed onto the guy and used momentum to propel him. Shoulder first, the guy slammed into a nearby tree. Since the pine tree clustered with dozens of others, it was tall and skinny. The frame cracked in half with the blow.

Colin popped to his feet before the guy could rebalance from the impact.

With the rage of an angry bull, Colin dove into the man…into who he could now see was Richard. An animal-like growl tore from Colin's throat as he took a blow to the face. His head snapped back and he instantly knew that he was going to feel that later. He had several inches of height and a lot more muscle on Richard. For his size, the guy threw a decent punch. Colin would give him that, and that was all he'd give.

Both men tumbled to the ground. Colin hopped to his feet first and threw a punch, connecting with the side of Richard's head. He ducked—about a second too late—and rolled.

Colin followed and then his legs were swept out from underneath him as Richard spun around.

The ground was cold and hard. Colin's shoulder took the brunt of the fall, and that was also going to hurt later. Right now, Colin's adrenaline pumped and all he could think about was stopping Richard.

With a couple seconds of a head start, Richard was retreating down the hill by the time Colin got to his feet. There was no use trying to use his backup weapon. There were too many trees in the way to get off a clean shot. So, he started down after Richard.

There could be a trap set up, so Colin needed to stop Richard. *Now.*

Anger and rage fueled Colin's movements.

Pouring on the speed, Colin dove down the hill, aiming at Richard, who was running at a decent clip. He couldn't outrun Colin. Richard was about to find that out as Colin made contact just below the man's knees.

Richard fell backward and on top of Colin. The two, connected by momentum, rolled down the hill out of control.

First came a *ker-plunk* sound and then the shock of freezing water. Colin gasped a second before his head submerged. If that had happened a second sooner, he'd be in trouble. He needed to get his bearings and get the hell out of the water.

At this temperature, he estimated that he had roughly two minutes before his muscles would weaken and slow down since he wore no protective clothing. He could already feel the effects of the cold in his hands and fingers. They were going numb. It wouldn't be long before his arms and legs felt the impact, too.

He kicked until his head broke the surface. The shoreline wasn't too far. He searched for signs of Rancic. Damn it, this would be too easy of an out for him. The man needed to pay for what he'd done.

With heavy arms, Colin swam until he could stand. He could barely feel his limbs by the time he pushed to standing. His arms were already numbing by the time he heaved himself up and out of the water.

His breath came out in bursts as he skimmed the top of the water for any sign of Richard. Disappointment settled in when he saw nothing. This area was dark and even though Colin's eyes had long ago adjusted, it was still difficult to see clearly. He'd left his cell phone at the campsite, which was a good fifty yards uphill. Shouting wouldn't do any good, but he did it anyway.

A shot was fired, echoing down the mountain and the blood in Colin's veins froze. The entire operation had exploded in a nanosecond and Colin could only pray everyone was okay above him. He had to trust that his brothers could handle it. He briefly thought about Melissa being up there alone in the gift shop. At least Rancic was in the water. There was no way Colin could leave the area until the man surfaced.

Colin's body began shaking. Wearing cold, wet clothes would cause his body to continue to decline, so he stripped off his shoes, followed by his jeans and his shirt. He fired off a few push-ups to warm his muscles as he kept his gaze focused on the surface of the water.

Not a minute had passed when Rancic's head surfaced. He'd managed to swim to the opposite bank and was pulling himself out of the water. That was at least thirty feet away. Colin popped up. He could take advantage of the fact that Richard's muscles would be cold. He was moving slowly and that gave Colin the advantage. He recalled Melissa flinching when he made a move toward her and the nightmare to give him an edge. Anger boiled through him when he added his daughter to the equation.

Rancic was on his knees, pushing off the ground by the time Colin reached him. Not sparing a second, Colin threw a punch.

Richard dropped down to the ground after it connected with his jaw. Another jab to his nose and blood squirted.

In the next second, Colin pinned Richard down. Something, a knife or sharp stick, sliced through Colin's right thigh. At least he still had feeling in his legs. He took it as a good sign and pushed on, biting back a curse as he took another swing at Rancic.

Colin wrestled the weapon out of the man's hand…a knife, and then tossed the blade into the water.

Cold was taking hold and Colin's body trembled.

"You think this is over. It's not," Rancic bit out. "You heard the shots. My family is taking care of that lying slut you love so much."

It took everything inside Colin not to grab hold of the man's neck and squeeze until there was no air left in his lungs. Death was too easy.

"You need to know before you spend the rest of your life in prison that Angelina is my daughter, not yours," Colin ground out through his anger. Since Richard was so big on family, he should know that Angelina was an O'Brien and would never be a Rancic.

Richard squirmed underneath Colin who had the guy trapped with his powerful thighs. "You should save your energy because you're not going anywhere except jail."

Based on his reaction, Colin had scored a direct hit.

"How can you be so sure?" Richard said, and there was a twitch in his voice that belied his words.

"Do the math. Melissa was already pregnant when you blackmailed her into marriage," Colin said, his anger rising at thinking about what she'd endured at the hands of this man. His fists clenched and released as he continued to give reasons as to why he shouldn't wring this guy's neck. A quick snap and Colin could erase Richard's existence. And that would feel incredible for a few seconds. But that would end Richard's misery at living out the rest of his life in jail before it even started. "It's the only reason she didn't leave you from the get-go. She wouldn't risk our child."

Richard made a move to knock Colin off him. Colin fisted his hand and belted Richard. His jaw snapped right and he spit blood.

Colin could hear footsteps thundering from behind and voices that he recognized as his brothers'. He listened for the sweet sound of Melissa's voice and tensed when he didn't hear it. He refused to give Rancic the satisfaction of seeing his fear.

"You're about to be arrested and face your crimes. Know this. If you or anyone you know ever messes with my family again from either side of the bars that you're about to spend a very long time getting to know, there won't be a place on earth that you can hide from me," Colin said through clenched teeth.

Richard sneered. "We'll see about that."

It took pretty much everything Colin had inside him at that moment not to put his hands around that man's neck and choke the life out of him for what he'd done to Melissa. He wasn't an impulsive guy. And being a good person meant doing the right thing and allowing justice to be served.

"Put your hands in the air where we can see them," an authoritative voice said from behind. Colin knew that tone would come from someone in law enforcement.

Colin complied, continuing to pin Richard while giving him the leeway he needed to put his own arms where officers could see them.

Richard's right hand fisted.

"I wouldn't try anything stupid if I were you," Colin said. "Or maybe not. How about you give them a reason to shoot. There's nothing I'd like to see more than you bleeding out right here."

Richard lifted his hands above his head where officers could see them.

"That's my brother." Joshua's voice was a welcomed relief. Colin's gaze snapped to his brother, who was pointing at Colin as another officer ran toward him.

Colin, arms high, eased off Richard as an officer rushed to them.

"Is she okay?" Colin asked.

"Yes," Joshua said, his gaze intent on Colin's right leg.

"Everyone else?" Colin asked. He was starting to get very cold.

"We're good," Joshua said. "The others are giving statements to law enforcement while Rancic's brother and buddies are being tucked into the backs of cruisers. It's over."

The officer forced Richard onto his stomach, facing the ground, and then jerked his arms up high behind him. Zip cuffs were on a few seconds later as the officer's knee jabbed into Richard's back. The officer seemed unfazed by Richard's threats of a lawsuit.

The officer held out a hand with a concerned expression. "Can you move?"

Colin followed the officer's line of sight to the blood streaming out of the top of his thigh.

"That's gonna leave a mark," Colin quipped as he heard the officer radio for medical treatment.

Joshua dropped to Colin's side a few seconds later, urging him to lie on his back.

And then Melissa was there, her beautiful face looking at him, her cheeks streaked with tears.

"It's cold," Colin said, and he could feel his teeth chatter.

"He needs something, blankets, coats, whatever you've got," she said, keeping her gaze on him. "I need you, Colin. Angelina needs you. You stay with us, okay."

A few seconds later warm blankets were being placed around him as Joshua worked on Colin's leg. A belt tightened around his upper thigh.

"I'm not going anywhere, sweetheart," Colin said to her. "No more tears. You're safe now."

"That should hold until we can get medical evacuation," Joshua said.

Colin looked over at Richard, whose face was covered in his own blood. Colin was pretty sure he'd busted the guy's nose.

"He can't hurt you anymore," he said as he shivered harder. His limbs were too heavy to move.

"Colin," she said as he was being lifted onto a stretcher.

The sound of her sweet voice was the last thing he heard before everything went black.

Chapter Eighteen

Melissa paced. She couldn't even look at Joshua, Tyler or Austin. All three of them wore the same expression that she felt inside…panic.

Colin had looked so white, except for his lips. They'd been blue. And he'd looked so weak.

She twisted her fingers together and took another walk around the Jeep.

Seeing Richard in the backseat of a cruiser after believing for so long that she'd never be free of him almost felt unreal. Justice would finally be served for all the families he'd hurt, for the law enforcement officer he'd shot, and for Tommy. Her heart still hurt for Marshal Davis's family and she wanted to do something for them. The least she could do was organize a scholarship fund for his children. His wife shouldn't have to worry about money after everything she'd been through. Melissa would reach out to her.

Richard was finally going to get exactly what he deserved, and she could only pray that prison wouldn't be kind to him.

An EMT walked toward her.

"Ma'am," he said. His nametag read PHILLIP.

"Yes." Her heart leapt to her throat.

"He's asking for you," Phillip said, motioning for her to follow him.

She glanced at his brothers as she hurried behind Phillip. It had to be a good sign that he was talking. She'd take what she could get.

Melissa had expected to feel differently as she watched the cruiser pull away with Richard in the back. She'd thought she'd feel lighter somehow. Except that she didn't. Not while Colin lay on a stretcher being worked on by two EMTs.

Her life had blown up before her eyes. She knew that Colin could never truly trust her again, but she loved him with all her heart and he had to be okay.

"You were so cold," she said, her chest squeezing at seeing him on that stretcher, wrapped in thick blankets.

"I'll be warmer if you'll slip under the covers with me," he said with that wry grin that was so charming. His gaze fixed on a spot behind her.

She turned in time to see Phillip standing there.

"Can you give us a few minutes of privacy?" Colin asked.

"Sure," Phillip said. "As long as you stay put."

"Where am I going to go?" Colin relented, sounding a little like a kid who'd just been told to sit in the corner.

"Okay, then." Phillip closed the doors.

"Come closer," Colin said to Melissa.

She scooted toward him on the bench, fighting back tears.

"I was serious about you joining me in here," he said, lifting the blanket. "Phillip said I'd warm up faster using body heat."

Before she could respond, he was tugging on her arm. She made a move to join him, her gaze freezing on the white bandage covering his right thigh.

She gasped. "Colin."

"It's all right. Barely a scratch," he said.

"You've always been a bad liar, Colin," Melissa said. It was true. He'd been much better at telling the truth.

"It'll heal in a few days," he said nonchalantly.

Melissa eased onto the gurney. He pulled

her close, her back against his strong chest. He shivered as he wrapped his arms around her.

"Are you sure this is a good idea?" she asked, not wanting to make his injuries worse.

"Phillip offered to climb in but I told him that I'd rather have you in here," he quipped. His easy charm had always been good at making her laugh when she shouldn't.

"I'm concerned about you, Colin."

"I know," he said against her neck before planting a kiss there.

A sensual shiver ran down her back and the mood shifted.

"I'm pretty sure Phillip wouldn't approve of you exerting too much energy right now," she said, melting against his body.

"Phillip doesn't know what's best for me." Colin's lips trailed down the sensitive spots along her neck.

"We need to be serious for a minute. I need to know that you're okay. I was so scared," she said.

"You're safe now," he said. "It's over."

The force of those words hit her like a physical punch. Richard was being hauled off in the back of a cruiser. He was going to go to jail for the rest of his life. The man who'd shot and killed Marshal Davis would never see the outside of prison gates. The man who had tortured her for a long year and stripped away everyone she loved couldn't hurt her anymore.

His top men, along with his brother, were being arrested at that exact moment, and Angelina would grow up away from the shadow of that horrible man.

Melissa couldn't stem her tears. She just lay there, Colin's arms around her, her strength. Her comfort.

Angelina would get to grow up knowing her real father.

She heard a noise outside the ambulance and gasped.

"It's okay. I'm here," Colin said, reassuring her.

But for how long?

Her life was a mess and even though he knew about Angelina and the two of them had shared many moments that gave her a spark of hope for a future, the bottom line was that he would never trust her again.

Richard had won, after all.

Nothing in her life made sense without Colin.

"I'll be right back." She slipped out of the covers and climbed out of the ambulance.

Colin shouted after her but she ignored him. He would be okay. His family was safe. Richard was going to jail.

Melissa could go home to her daughter and begin to build a new life. She needed to figure out her next steps for her father, and she needed to get a job to support her family. She could return to the town she loved and her daughter could finally claim her birthright. Angelina O'Brien. The name sounded right.

She glanced around. The O'Briens were busy packing up.

They were going home. Why did that make her feel so empty?

Melissa needed to get it together because there was a lot to think about.

She heard arguing coming from the ambulance and turned in time to see Phillip helping Colin out of the back.

"What's going on?" she asked.

"I was hoping you could convince him to let us give him a ride to the hospital," Phillip said, looking flustered.

"I'm fine," Colin said, hopping on his left leg.

Phillip had to hold on to him in order to keep him from falling.

"Once he makes up his mind, it's pretty difficult to convince him otherwise," Melissa said, grateful they were all standing there smiling.

"Then, I'm all done here," Phillip said. "Bandages need to be changed every day."

"Will do," Colin said before thanking Phillip and then shaking his hand.

"Are you sure this is a good idea?" she asked Colin.

"You took off so fast a minute ago," he said. "I didn't get a chance to tell you that Phillip was about to release me."

Phillip shot Colin a look, excused himself and then disappeared around the side of the ambulance.

"It's over. I have to try to pick up the pieces." She couldn't look up at him. The thought of going on to a life without him pierced her chest. He'd be in her life at least partially because of Angelina. That was something. She needed to change the subject before she lost it again. "I was just thinking about trying to kick-start a fund-raiser for Marshal Davis's family."

"I already made a call to have a scholarship set up for his kids," he said. "I'd like to make sure his widow is taken care of, as well."

"That was really sweet of you." She was grateful to have the O'Brien name involved. Colin could get the job done with one call. "I know that money can't bring back or replace a husband and father, but I'd like to do as much as possible to ease the burden on the family."

"Good. We can work together on it," he said.

"Colin, I know you and I know that your trust in me has been…broken." She kept her eyes focused on the ground so she wouldn't start crying. There'd been enough tears in the past year to last a lifetime.

Colin took a step toward her and then lifted her chin until their eyes met.

"I want you to look at me when I say this because it's important to me," he started.

She took in a deep breath.

"I love you, Melissa," he said. "That won't change."

That last word echoed in her mind. *Change.* Didn't that encompass so much of her life, of her?

"But you have?" she asked.

"I've always loved you. It's always been you," he said, and her heart pounded inside her chest. "But I respect you even more now for what you've suffered."

There was so much love and respect in his gaze.

"I couldn't be more proud of you," he said.

"I…I didn't think you'd understand," she said.

"There's a big part of me that still wishes you'd trusted me enough to tell me earlier, but you put our daughter first and I could never be angry with you for doing that," he said. "You're an amazing mother and I love you even more after seeing you with Angelina. I know that everything you did, all your actions, were meant to protect her. And in your heart you believed that you were protecting me and my family, too."

Melissa's heart flowered with hope for a future together as a family. "Will you ever trust me again?"

"Will you ever fully trust me?" he asked.

"Me?"

"I may have acted on impulse in the past and been immature as all hell sometimes, but that all stopped when I met you, Melissa." Colin wrapped his arms around her waist and she leaned into him. "You're the only person I want to be with other than a three-month-old big-eyed beauty who looks a lot like you."

"Can we start over?" she asked, hopeful for the future she never thought would be within reach.

"I don't want a new beginning," he said. "I love you now as much as I ever did, and I'd like to pick up where we left off, planning our wedding."

She tilted her head up and kissed him.

When she finally pulled back, he looked straight into her eyes and said, "You and that little girl are my family and I want to make it

Get 2 Free Books,
Plus 2 Free Gifts—
just for trying the
Reader Service!

Get 2 Free Books,
Plus 2 Free Gifts—
just for trying the Reader Service!

Get 2 Free Books,
Plus <u>2</u> Free Gifts—
just for trying the Reader Service!

"On the way, we need to call Carolina to thank her for bringing you to the Spring Fling," Colin said to her.

She beamed up at him.

Colin linked his and Melissa's fingers. "Are you ready to go home to our daughter?"

"Yes, I am. I want to go home."

* * * * *

Look for the next book in USA TODAY
Bestselling Author Barb Han's
CATTLEMEN CRIME CLUB *miniseries,*
TEXAS SHOWDOWN,
available next month.

And don't miss the previous titles in the
CATTLEMEN CRIME CLUB *series:*

STOCKYARD SNATCHING
DELIVERING JUSTICE
ONE TOUGH TEXAN
TEXAS-SIZED TROUBLE

Available now from Harlequin Intrigue!

official so the three of us can be together for the rest of our lives."

"I do, too," was all she said, all she had to say, before he pulled her in tight and kissed her again.

"I love you, Colin O'Brien. I should've trusted you before but I do now. I'm trusting you with our child and with all my heart."

"Then there's only one more thing I need you to say." He took a knee, wincing in pain.

"Don't hurt yourself," she said, but he waved her off. This time, it didn't feel like a fairy tale, like something unreal or out of reach. Colin was right there. And a lifetime with him was within her grasp.

Melissa touched his face as he asked the words again.

"Will you marry me?" he asked.

"Yes."

"Hey, you two," Austin called over to them.

"Whatever you have to say, it can wait. I'm about to kiss my future wife." Colin stood up—with great effort and some wincing—and took Melissa in his arms. He then gave her the kind of kiss that stole her breath.

All three of his brothers clapped.

"Well, when you two are done there's a jet sitting on a tarmac at Denver Airport waiting to take us home," Austin quipped.